A Savage Love

Aryanna

**Ca$h Presents
A Savage Love
A Novel by *Aryanna***

A Savage Love

Lock Down Publications
P.O. Box 1482
Pine Lake, Ga 30072-1482

Visit our website at **www.lockdownpublications.com**

First Edition November 2016
Printed in the United States of America

Lock Down Publications
Like our page on Facebook: Lock Down Publications
@www.facebook.com/lockdownpublications.ldp
Cover design and layout by: Dynasty's Cover Me
Book interior design by: Shawn Walker
Edited by: Cassandra Barrett-Sims

ACKNOWLEDGEMENTS

Father God, to be here again is a testament of your blessings and grace, and I'm truly thankful.

I have to thank my beautiful Belinda Diane for the constant love and support, and that occasional kick in the ass when I needed it. LOL! I love you!

I have to thank Micaela "Kiddoodle" Lorraine, and Elizabeth "Grumpybear" Ann, for loving me when I needed it the most, and for keeping me focused, because I promised you the world. LOL!

I have to thank my mother, Carmel, and my mom, Donna—both of you love me differently, but it's what I need and I'm so grateful to have you both in my life.

I have to thank my God-mother, Monica, for all of your continuous love and support, and I promise you it gets greater later! As soon as I can I will, and you know this.

I have to thank my fans who are my family, because without you I'm nothing—your support means the world to me.

This book is a little different, but I know you'll love it! I have to thank all my little people even though you're not old enough to read my content yet. LOL! Just know our future looks brighter than ever, and yours will always be secure.

I have to thank my LDP family for being what I need when I need it, even when I'm impatient. Thank you for all the love, and your constant support— you helped create a monster! LOL!

I have to thank my sistah, Reds Johnson— you acknowledged me and you didn't have to— that gesture alone means so much more to me, knowing I was even on your radar. With the catalog of work, you have its humbling, but definitely motivation! The love is real and I give it all back to you, I promise. Our collaboration is a must! LOL!

I have to thank my sistah, Coffee, for the support of me and mine through the good and the bad. I love you for that, and for taking my shit because I know I'm on your nerves! LOL!

I have to thank everyone who supports me, and stands behind me, not just with my writing, but in my life, period. I'm not easy to love, but you stick by me, and that means the world is ours.

As always, I have to close with special thanks to my baby girl, Aryanna, for her existence. I am because you are, and I love you more each day for that. I GOTCHU!

LDP we in here, and the game is ours!!

DEDICATION

This book is dedicated to: Kiara Cheyenne, because you are everything!

Aryanna

CHAPTER ONE
'Bout that Life

"Visitor for Thompson," the female called out, as she looked around the room.

Closing my diary, I placed it inside my purse, and prepared to be violated. Although it was something I would never get used to, I could only imagine how the nigga's felt who suffered the same indecency day after day.

"Ms. Preston," I said, letting her know it was my name she'd summoned.

After getting her attention I proceeded with the usual protocol, and gave her my I.D.

Once she glanced at it briefly, she led me to a windowless room where the search would take place. Being familiar with the routine, I didn't bother waiting for further instructions. Instead, I emptied the contents of my purse onto the table, and removed my shoes.

"I see you've been here before," she said.

I didn't bother replying, but I gave her an insincere smile, hoping the gesture would be enough to get through the process as quickly as possible. Even though I was into females, I didn't relish the thought of this old broad rubbing on me, not even a little.

"You here to visit your father?" she asked.

My first thought was to tell her to stay out of my damn business, but the look in her grandmother-like eyes told me she was simply trying to make polite conversation. It was a change from the stank-ass attitude I usually got from the thirsty bitches who worked here at Lorton Prison, so it caught me off guard.

"Nah, I'm here to see my man," I replied, without offering additional information.

"Oh," she said in a sarcastic tone of voice

I felt myself on the verge of losing it on this woman because her response sounded judgmental against me and mine. I had dealt with enough opinions in the street about me and my choices of men, and I really didn't need someone else offering me their two-cents. I'd heard it all before anyway, comments like, how beautiful and smart I was, and how I could do better.

It was funny how most mufuckers offering advice or had opinions on my relationship were either single, or miserable in their own relationship. *And I'm supposed to listen to them? Yea, right,* I thought. I wasn't so blind that I couldn't see the truth when it was staring me right in the face.

I was a bad bitch standing five feet one, with a sweet honey complexion. My titties were firm and round, and they sat up just right. My stomach was as flat as an ironing board, and I'd been blessed with an ass that would stop traffic more than evening rush hour. And whether people realized it or not, I also had a brain; my upcoming graduation from high school was evidence of that, not to mention my 4.0 GPA.

I could have any nigga I wanted, but people didn't seem to understand the key part of that statement meant *any nigga "I" wanted,* not who they thought was best for me.

Lorenzo was my man, and he didn't have to be perfect, as long as he was perfect for me. And what type of chick abandons her man when he catches a bid? If it ain't life it ain't long, and I had my baby's back to the fullest.

Putting all my belongings back in my purse, I stored it in one of visitor lockers they gave to all visitors then I put the locker key in my pocket.

Next, came the inspection of my shoes, as if I would fuck up my Jordan's for some dumb shit like trying to smuggle shit in. Once that was done, the officer patted me down and made me lift up my bra and shake it, to ensure there was nothing illegal in there. Finally, she gave the all clear sign for the backdoor to slide open, and I was let through.

"How old are you sweetheart?" she asked.

"I'm 18, why?" I replied, getting annoyed once again.

"I just… Well, it's not my place to say this, but from one woman to another, please, don't spend your life in places like this. Not even as a visitor," she added.

Before I could respond the door slid shut, and I was left looking back at my own reflection. I had so many things on the tip of my tongue, but seeing my man was more important.

I quickly made my way into the run down gymnasium that served as the visitation room. I was more than anxious to see the smile on Zo's face, and more than ready to feel his strong arms around me. Zo was short for Lorenzo, and it was the name the streets knew him by.

As I looked around, I quickly spotted him sitting in the back of the room, off in a corner. As always, his eyes were focused towards the door anticipating my entrance. When our eyes met, I felt the tingling sensation start in my stomach, as it always did, before working its way down, causing my pussy to throb in sync with the rhythm of my heartbeat.

No other nigga had ever had this kind of effect on me, not ever. There was just something about Lorenzo Thompson that made my heart race every time I was in his presence. He wasn't a pretty boy, but he had that rugged kind of sex appeal. I'd never hype his head up by telling him this, but his dick game was definitely on point! *Whenever we made love, he took me to places I'd never dreamed of going. My mind would be lost in total bliss and the orgasms would come fast, back to back. Umph,* the thought alone made my pussy jump.

Lorenzo towered over me at six feet two, and he weighed at least 200lbs— his body was cut up like a one eighth block of dope, from working out the past 2 years. He was so black, he was damn near blue, a complexion most women would consider black and lovely, and he had the whitest teeth I'd ever seen on a man.

I'd first met him about three years back at a go-go party at a little club called Kebox in D.C. The Junkyard Band had come to party and I was determined not to miss out, so, like always, I showed up, and showed out.

Zo had come to party too, but before he got inside he had to straighten a nigga in the parking lot. I hopped out of my cousin's Mazda 929 looking like new money in a strapless green Gucci dress, with the matching fuck-me pumps. I noticed a crowd gathered around and wondered what was going on. As I made my way to the scene, there was Zo beating the skin off a mufucka's face. As wrong as it was, seeing him in action, the shit turned me on.

I didn't think he was paying any attention to me at the time, but somehow during the night, he ended up with my number which led to a lot of late night, early morning conversations. From that point on, we started kickin' it together every now and then. I mean, I didn't really have a lot of time to party because my school work was my main priority, and so was my money.

Going to Dunbar High School offered me a chance to get my education, and to also pimp the weed I was getting from my uncle. I was definitely making moves.

At the age of 18 Zo was a hood legend around 37th and Minnesota, and he was a big homie for 92 Hoover Crips. He had enemies, but he also had power and respect, and that shit was sexy as hell to me. He didn't abuse his power and his street mentality intrigued me.

We got to know each other for a couple months, and once we took it to the next level we were inseparable. Unfortunately, he caught a gun case, and he was hit with a 5 year bid.

I thought I would die! I mean, my world was, once again, coming unglued. After losing my father to a sudden illness when I was just 9, and losing my mother to the crack pipe at 10, I had more or less given up on depending on people— that is, until I met Zo. So, to turn around and lose him to the system had me crying tears I never thought would end. Then, one day during our very first visit we had a serious heart to heart, and it really helped me put things into perspective. He reminded me that this was the life we'd chosen to live. So, from that moment forward, I put my big girl panties on and held my nigga down like a real bitch was supposed to, without question or hesitation.

Lately, I'd been thinking maybe it was time to take a different approach to the way we'd been making our money. Zo would be home soon if his parole was approved and I wanted to make sure, if and when he got out, he'd stay out.

***

As soon as I was close enough I leapt into his arms, as he simultaneously lifted me off my feet. Without wasting another minute, I locked one onto his big juicy lips. We kissed as if it had been years, instead of weeks, since we'd last seen one another. His lips tasted like cherry Kool-Aid and weed, which just happened to be two of my favorite things, and I tried to inhale his essence in that one kiss. I could tell he wanted me as much as much I wanted him, because his response damn near made me cum instantly. When he lowered me back down to the floor, my knees were so weak they were shaking. Normally, I despised weak women, but if truth-be-told, I couldn't hide my own weakness even if I tried; I loved me some him, and I'd do whatever I had to for him.

"What's good, Slim?" he asked, with that same sexy smile he'd always give me during or visitation times.

"It's all good now, baby, since I'm in your arms," I replied, staring deeply into his dark brown eyes.

"Took you long enough," he said, with mock irritation.

I jabbed him playfully in the stomach before standing on my tippy toes for another kiss.

"You want somethin' to eat?" I asked.

"You know what I like," he replied, winking at me before sitting in the foldout chair.

I couldn't hide my smile as I walked to the vending machines up front to get my baby his food. As usual I felt the heat of the stares from all the other niggas, and their bitches, but I never worried about being disrespected. I could definitely handle my own, but Zo wasn't about to let anybody fuck with me. He wasn't one to be fucked with, and everybody knew it.

Once I'd made it to the vending machines, I got him two cheeseburgers, two bags of chips and a soda, and got a pizza for myself. After warming up all the food, I took it back to the little table that sat in between our chairs, and laid it out on the paper plates he'd gotten from the guards.

I really didn't feel like eating, but if I didn't then I'd have to hear his mouth about me not taking care of myself. He was gangsta in front of the masses, but to me he was just a big teddy bear who constantly fussed over me.

"So, what's been up, babe?" he asked, taking a bite of his burger.

"Same ole' shit, work and school," I answered honestly.

"You excited about graduation?" he asked.

"Hell yeah!" I replied, excitement evident in my tone.

"I'm proud of you, you know that right? I mean not many people come from this side and manage to stay clear of all its bullshit. So many mufuckas is dying in this city, even in here, we hear 'bout how crazy the streets of D.C. gettin'. Just to know my baby out there gettin' money *and* a education, shit yeah, I'm hella proud of you, Makayla."

His words touched me, ensuring me of just how much he respected me, because not a lot of men considered women their

12

equal. Even with the new millennium approaching, Zo never once talked down to me.

"I love you baby," I said, leaning over to kiss him.

"I love you too," he replied sincerely.

We continued eating our food and enjoying each other's company for about an hour. Not too long after, I noticed that familiar, restless look come across his face which often appeared as our visitation time came closer to ending.

I knew he loved me, but my man was a mover and a shaker. I also knew being confined and being told what to do, and when to do it, was taking a toll on what he had been accustomed to on the streets.

"So, tell me what we lookin' like out there right now," he said, leaning over the table so those close to us couldn't eavesdrop.

"We got about $90,000 put away. You know Love from the K. St. crew out there by my aunt's house, right?"

"Yeah, what about him?" he asked curiously.

"Well, he said I can get 'em whole for $17,500 and he'll give me I St., 4 St., and L St. to work."

I could tell Zo was contemplating heavily because this was a huge move I was bringing to the table; it was the difference between part-time grinding, and full-time hustling. The look on his face showed his indecisiveness. I knew he was worried because the streets were unforgiving and uncompromising, which meant death or prison would be your destination ninety percent of the time. I wanted so badly for us to be that rare ten percent.

"Let me think about that for a minute," he finally said. "I go up for parole next week so until then, just lay low and catch the money already comin' at you. Other than that, what's up with the homies?"

"Face and C-Will came past the house last night to blow a couple blunts wit' me, they out there groovin' real hard."

"Cool. Tell 'em to be by a phone later on tonight so I can call and holla at 'em. So what you gettin' into tonight?"

"Nothin' much, probably just chill wit' my girl, Jessica."

The mention of my girlfriend's name caused this goofy ass grin to come across his face. He was cool with me and her fuckin', but I knew his fantasy was to have us both at the same time. He was smart enough not to suggest it, because he knew I would beat his ass up, right here in the visiting room. "Eatin ain't cheatin," he said, laughing at his own humor.

"Whatever," I responded. "How much money should there be in the P.O. Box?" I asked, changing the subject.

"Should be about five grand," he answered without hesitation, "and I've got another grand on me," he added. "How much you bring?"

"I brought a ounce. You want me to go 'head and get it out?"

Zo glanced around the room quickly, making sure the coast was clear. Once he was sure no one was paying any attention to us, he looked at me and nodded a quick nod. "Yeah, go 'head and make that move," he said, after giving me the signal.

I kissed him quickly and made my way to the bathroom to get the ounce of cocaine out of my pussy. I tried hard not to think about what the consequences would be if I were to get caught. Not only was what I doing illegal, but I had basically brought an illegal substance onto prison grounds, which was no doubt a felony. He promised me I wouldn't have to do it too many more times and he'd said it was only temporary.

The two of us had set a goal of $250,000, and the money we'd make would be used to relocate and start our lives over. Our plan was to leave Washington D.C. and all its drama behind us. It made more sense to sell dope in prison when compared to selling it on the streets, and the money was a helluva lot better. So, being a true ride or die, I did what I had to do for us, and prayed we could beat the odds.

14

Walking into the dimly lit bathroom, I made my way inside the stall, trying not to breath in the funk of shit and piss mixed with worn out pussy. Once the door was locked I pulled my jeans half way down, squatted, and pulled the condom out from inside me. Most chicks had to worry about packing, but my man had given me the game of how to turn a little into a lot. All it took was a quarter roll, two condoms, and the rest was common sense, for real.

I tucked the pack in my bra and pulled my panties and jeans up. Just as I was getting ready to unlock the stall, I heard the bathroom door open. *Oh, shit,* I thought, hoping I wasn't busted.

"Mac," Lorenzo whispered, scaring the shit out of me.

I flipped the lock on the stall door and opened it to find him standing there grinning like a fat kid at a buffet.

"Boy, what the hell are you doin'? We gonna get cau..."

"Shhh," he said, cutting my words off midsentence.

He pushed me back inside of the stall, and flipped the lock, before pinning me to the wall with a powerful kiss. My mind kept screaming that I should be worried about getting caught, but my pussy was wetter than it had been in years. The feeling of being wrapped in my man's embrace was indescribable, and I'd missed it so much it brought tears to my eyes.

"We gotta hurry babe, turn around and bend over," he said.

Before I could do what he'd asked he had already unbuttoned my jeans and shove his hands inside my panties. I could feel my juices dripping down his fingers when he used them to part my pussy lips, exploring inside of me. I hadn't had any dick since our last time together, which was two years ago. To say I was tight was a serious understatement, but I wanted him inside me in the worst way.

I bent over and grabbed the handicapped pole attached to the bathroom wall for leverage, as he snatched my jeans down to my ankles. I opened my mouth to tell him to be gentle, but I didn't get the warning out before he'd shoved inside of me with enough force to rip me in half.

"Baby," I managed to croak out, hoping he'd take heed and take it a little slower.

"I gotchu, Slim," he said pulling his dick all the way out of me before feeding it to me again an inch at a time.

After two more strokes, I felt my pussy spasm before I came harder than I thought humanly possible.

"Daddy, I've missed you," I told him, pushing back on him, as he began to pound harder inside me.

The feeling of his powerful hands gripping my hips made me cum again, and I could taste the blood from my lip as I bit it to keep from screaming. It felt like he was in my stomach, and I loved it, I loved him.

"Oh, shit, Mac, I'm 'bout to cum," he growled.

He grabbed me tighter and began to fuck me faster and harder, almost lifting me off my feet with each stroke.

"Me too," I panted, clinching his dick with my pussy muscles, as I felt the heat of his cum shooting inside of me. The sensation made me wish we were at home so we could start all over again.

He pulled out of me and turned me around to face him. I could feel his love and hunger for me, and his eyes held the look of a swirling storm.

"I love you, Makayl," he whispered in my ear, "our time apart is almost over, and soon, I'll be home to give you the future I know you deserve."

"You promise?" I whispered back.

Without answering, he sealed his promise with a kiss so soft and gentle, the tears I'd been holding back finally spilled over. This was my man, my king, and nothing could change that.

CHAPTER TWO
Everyday I'm Hustlin'

It felt good to wake up with a smile on my face, still smelling like yesterday's surprise encounter with Zo. Damn, I loved that man. I was already counting the days until he came home, and we could finally get back to building our future together. In the meantime, I had to stay focused and on my grind in more ways than one, because a bitch had to get ahead when she was doing for herself.

Hopping in the shower, I began analyzing and thinking about the overall plan and how things would fall into place.

Zo would be going up for parole at the end of the week, and if it was granted he'd be home by July 1st. While I waited, I needed to make as much money as I could to get us as close as possible to the quarter million goal we had in mind.

During my lunch break, I needed to go scoop up the five grand from our office box. I'd put that with the $800 I had from the money he'd given me the previous day. The $200 charge for our 10 minutes of privacy was well worth it, and little did he know, I'd be surprising him again this weekend with some more of this good pussy. My body awakened at the thought of his touch, but I shook my head in hopes of reorganizing my thoughts so business would come first.

After I handling my drops and pickups at school, I'd need to arrange a meeting with a nigga known as Success and see what the play was for Jessica's B-Day party.

Success was pimp out of Milwaukee who kept some of the finest hoes seen from here to Vegas. I planned to do it big for my baby's 21st b-day, so calling him was a must. After I handled the mall in VA "Work hard play hard was the motto."

I took my time washing my hair even though I knew it'd make me late for school. What did it matter with graduation only a few weeks away, plus I couldn't have my locks stinkin' and shit.

Snapping me out of my thoughts, Jessica called from outside the bathroom door, "Mac?"

"Yeah," I answered.

"Come on, babe, I gotta take a shower before work," she said impatiently.

I hated being rushed and this was just one of the many things that made me leery about us living together in the first place. I fucked with Slim tough though, and I loved the feel of her warm body next to mine at night. Maybe it was just time to move out of the two-bedroom apt. and find something that would give us our own space; I was definitely going to talk to Zo about it today when he called.

After a quick rinse, I shut the water off and pulled the curtain back to find a very naked Jessica standing there admiring her curves in the mirror. We were about the same height, but the similarities stopped there. I called her my chocolate drop because she was that Hershey Kiss kinda dark. Her ass wasn't as big as mine, but it was enough to hold onto and enjoy. Her titties were a perfect 36C cup and the most perfect set I'd ever had the pleasure of seeing or fondling, and her quarter sized nipples reminded me of tasty chocolate chips.

My own 40DDs hurt my back, but she loved them and we'd often spend time just lying in the bed touching each other until we couldn't stand it any longer. She rocked her hair short and kept it slicked down with styling gel, but I knew from personal experience it was still enough to run my fingers through and hold on to. To me, her face was her best feature. She had deep dimples in her cheeks, pearly white teeth, and eyes I could only describe as gun metal gray. She insisted I had the prettier eyes because mine were hazel green, but I disagreed because I'd inherited mine from being biracial, and hers were congenital.

She caught me observing her in the mirror and gave me that lazy smile that always did something to me. The reason we were so good together was because we'd always gotten along well, and when we did piss each other off, we never stayed mad with one another long.

"Sorry it took me so long babe, but you know you don't gotta go to work," I told her seriously.

"We've had this discussion, Sweetheart, I respect how you move, but you know that ain't how I get down," she replied.

I hated having to see her struggle for a little bit of nothing. But, I also understood her past experience with one particular dope boy had left her feeling some type of way; the way he died while living that life had literally traumatized her.

I took my towel from the rack, wrapped it around me, and stepped out of the shower. I kissed her on the forehead and gave her a hug before going back to my bedroom.

I quickly moisturized my body, put my panties and bra on, and grabbed a Baby Phat sweat suit from my closet. My pink Timbs matched the black and pink outfit perfectly. Once I was dressed, had my keys and backpack, I was out the door.

My first period class would start in 30 minutes, which meant I was gonna have to drive instead of taking the subway like I usually would.

My 98 money green Lexus LS 400 was a gorgeous sight as the sun rose over it, causing it to shine brighter than the stars on a moonlit night. This was my baby, my one extravagance. Even though I saved most of the money we made, and kept it clean, I wanted badly to throw some rims on this bad mufucka.

Always trying to stay ahead of my game, and knowing how the police watched and preyed, I felt like pimpin' my ride would draw too much attention, especially with the tint I already had on my windows. My favorite part of the car was the sound system. I had four twelve-inch crunch speakers in a box in the trunk, powered by two 1400 watt amps. My shit rattled, and you most definitely heard me before you saw me.

I hopped in and cranked *Life after Death*, which stayed in the system, nodding my head to the wisdom of Biggie's *Ten Crack Commandments*. I raced up M St. leaving southeast and entering southwest, needing to see my uncle Joe over on Half St. since he had the best weed outside Barry Farms. I knew he'd be out there at the corner store by Half St. and O because his philosophy was *"The early bird gets the worm,"* but the worm was early too.

I pulled up, and just as I'd expected he was posted up with a bottle of Thunderbird in his hand, talking to some chick who'd definitely seen better days. I gassed to the curb and lowered both my window and my music.

Knowing he'd spotted me before I'd even bent the corner there was no need to call him. I used the time waiting to crack a Philly blunt and roll a fatty up to get my mind where it needed to be for the day.

The lime green bud was sticky to the touch, but it was potent and that was all that mattered. To me, weed was the best thing ever invented. I knew I could make more money pimpin' coke or crack on the streets, but my appreciation of weed made me a better business woman when it came to sales. I didn't sell bullshit, and my quantity was always straight, so I kept a very loyal clientele, plus, if shit ever got ugly they wouldn't put my black ass under the penitentiary. I knew one of Biggies crack commandments was never get high on your own supply, but bud needed to be smoked. I hit my blunt and inhaled hard, enjoying the scorching feeling that only comes with blowing that good chronic out while trying not to choke.

"Morning, baby girl," my Uncle Joe said, leaning down inside my window.

He had a basketball player's height and build, with my daddy's mahogany complexion. His eyes were a piercing brown that didn't miss shit!

"Morning, Unc," I replied back, around a mouth full of smoke before passing him the blunt.

He hit it twice, quickly, never pausing in his constant observation of the streets he called home. Joe had been around since the rueful Edmonds' years, meaning, a lot of money had passed through his fingers, and a lot of street knowledge was floating around in his head.

"How's Zo?" he asked, passing the blunt back.

"He's maintaining, waiting and anticipating his parole hearing this week," I answered.

"Hopefully, he makes it so you can focus on what you need to be doing full-time, instead being out here with us scoundrels."

"Awww, Uncle Joe, you know I don't enjoy nobody's company more than yours," I said, meaning every word.

"See in my day...," he started before I butted in.

"As much as I'd love to hear one of your stories, I'm already running late for school," I said, glad I had a good excuse to avoid the lecture. I loved the man to death, but he wasn't used to a woman running the show.

"What you need?" he asked, already knowing why I was there.

"A pound," I said, simultaneously popping my trunk. Ordinarily I wouldn't tote this much by myself, but I'd only have it for a short time before it was sold.

"How much for personal use?" he questioned.

"The same," I replied as always.

He signaled one of his runners, and before you could get whistle out a chick was coming out of the alley from behind the store, carrying a Burberry bag.

"I'll bring you the money at lunch time, OK?" I confirmed.

21

"You know you good, baby girl, just be safe with all that shit," he said in a serious tone.

I assured him I would, and once my trunk was closed I pulled away from the curb and head to school. The weed had me mellow, causing me to switch from the metaphorical assassin, Biggie, to my girl, Aaliyah.

I cruised the rest of the way bumping, *One In a Million*, thinking and reminiscing about my baby and how things would be once he was home. It wasn't hard to envision my life as Mrs. Lorenzo Thompson because I knew he was the man I'd been waiting for my entire life. Hopefully, I'd only have to wait about five more weeks for my happily ever after to begin, especially since I needed some more of that good dick in a hurry.

I pulled into the student parking lot and turned the car off, before grabbing my diary out of my backpack. Poetry was my outlet, my main form of expression because it allowed me the vulnerability I wanted without the judgment people offered. It was the one positive thing my father passed along to me, but it had taken a while for me to hear that inner voice of truth, which allowed me to put my thoughts and feelings down on paper.

So, now I would write whenever the impulse struck, and at this very moment the love I felt for Zo was inspiring thoughts that had been jumping around in my head since yesterday. I opened my diary and paused briefly, as I allowed my heartfelt thoughts to dance around in my head. With a crooked smile spread across my face, I began writing the things I could see so vividly.

Where It Starts:

Smile for me baby. Do it seductively so when I look into your eyes I can peek at your soul and see me.

See us dancing slowly, completely captivated by the music between we.

The way your lips curve ever so slightly, the cross between smirk and sexiness somehow does it for me, and has me craving all the treasures that lie within.

The carvel suggestions of sin and sinner roll from my tongue on a whisper so only your ears hear what I want to happen here, and now.

Genuine smiles can't be faked, and the desire that takes up space in your eyes assures me the widening of your succulent lips as they approach mine is only the beginning of our adventure.

Time stands still, because we were meant for this moment, this uncensored joining of so much more than the physical.

As our tongues intertwine I feel the pull of your love on my soul, and my hands caress the firm lines of your body, making my need for you difficult to misinterpret.

Heightened senses allow me to feel my earth when your heart beat tilts on its axis, making the facts of something as simple as up and down take on new meaning.

I find myself on my back with you inside me, needing that in which only I can give.

We live in the moment of you taking me, and us moving to the tune of, give what you can take, but don't bite off more than you can chew.

It's not just making love, it's binding one soul to its counter-part, struggling to start finding the answer of what makes us crave this way so strongly.

Mmmm...

How long it's been since the two of us did this one thing, quenched the thirst and satisfied the appetite that imagining this beginning of love would bring to us.

So much more than lust this is, but the words to describe it are too complicated to formulate, because with each downward stroke, you're taking my breath away.

Our bodies rock like a fierce lullaby, sweetening the deeper I let you inside me as you rise and fall, rise and fall again, pushing me to the edge of sanity.

I can't hold back, I can't wait any longer, and then it ends, or does it?

You still move with purpose and a dazzling smile, so it's really the beginning again...

I closed my diary with an even bigger smile on my face. Everything I'd just written had come straight from the heart and soul, while thoughts of Zo pierced my heart as if I'd been shot by Cupid himself. After putting it in my backpack, I hopped out my ride into the beautiful, morning sunshine. I wasn't as late as I figured I'd be because there were still students moving around.

I had first period English which started my day off right because that was one of my favorite classes. I breezed through the halls speaking to those who were worth speaking to, while ignoring the hungry look in the eyes of niggas whose only interest was in what was in between my legs. It was crazy how after four years they still didn't get the fact that I wasn't some jump-off. The only mufucka who ever got some of this good-good was Zo, and that was because he'd taken the time to get to know me, and see what I'm *really* about.

I opened the door to my class, and heard some girl reading Romeo and Juliet. I made my way to my seat in the back without paying too much attention to the hole Mrs. Price was trying to stare through me. She couldn't stand to have her class interrupted, and I knew I'd be hearing about the shit later on.

"What up bitch?" My homegirl Teshia whispered, as I slid in the seat next to hers.

"Shit, I'm good. 'Sup with you?" I replied in a low tone.

"Wishing the weekend didn't have to end," she said, "girl, I was at the Ramada Inn with K.P and that shit was Hot!" she said in an animated tone. Her blue eyes twinkle like they always did when she was on some freak shit.

Teisha and I had been friends for about seven years, going back to my days on the streets of Hagerstown, MD. We were closer than friends, more like sisters, actually closer than me and my estranged siblings. I loved her to death, but she was full blown crazy!

First of all, she was a white girl who didn't know she was white, and that kept us in more fights than a little bit with the hood boogers around the way. She was only five feet five, and weighed a healthy 160lbs. I swear, it was all ass! And believe me she had a lot of black girls jealous. Her face was kinda plain with her mousy-brown hair, but she still turned plenty of heads, and she most definitely wasn't shy with the pussy. That is, until she settled down with K.P. She was tough and had a mouth on her, which more often than not resulted in a fight, but I had her back at all times. I was hated too for being mixed and gorgeous, not to mention, arrogant, so we bonded over that. Plus, her man and I did business together from time to time.

"Do I even wanna know what happened with your nasty ass?" I asked, laughing.

"Girlll, that mufucka licked my asshole and..."

"Nah, I don't wanna know!" I said, throwing my hands up and laughing harder.

"All I'ma say is, *when!* When the weekend was over he had to carry me to the car because I was no more good!" she said.

The smile on her face was all the evidence I needed to know she was reliving the moment in her mind.

"You go see Zo?" she asked, changing the subject.

"You know I did. Mmph, I love that man."

"I bet you do bitch. You got that good dick glow on you," she said with a devious smirk.

"Shhh, with your loud ass, I don't need everybody in my damn business," I said a little agitated.

"Well I'm definitely trying to be in your business, so spill it," she inquired.

I quickly recounted my weekend love session, trying to ignore the moisture forming in my panties from the memory of Zo being inside me invoked.

"Sounds hot," she said in her white girl voice, "when will he be home?"

"Hopefully, July 1st, and I can't wait."

"That's not a lot of time to get the kinda money you want, so what's the plan?"

"Well, I talked to Zo bout the offer Louie made and he said he'd think about it, but I'm ready to get to it."

"You know I'm with you 110%, Slim, just tell me what you need," she offered sincerely.

"For real?" I asked, although I knew she'd do whatever.

"Next question, bitch. You know I'm with you all the way on whatever, whenever."

It was really against my nature to go against what my baby wanted, but the more money I had when he got home, the less he'd have to be in the streets. Sometimes, you had to ask for forgiveness instead of permission.

"Can you and KP come to the house tonight?" I asked.

"What time?" She answered without hesitation.

"'Bout 8pm."

"Aight, cool. I'll let him know," she added, letting me know she'd be there.

"Bet, and tell him to come get this bud real quick. I'ma float him a pound for $1,000," I whispered to be sure no one could hear me.

"I gotchu," she replied, pulling out her two-way pager.

There was money to be made, and I was gonna make it. By any means necessary.

Aryanna

CHAPTER THREE
Surprise

First period was the only class me and Teshia had together, but we always hooked up for lunch. I was chillin' in my car conducting business on my two-way when she slumped in the seat beside me, attitude was written all over her face.

"What's wrong?" I asked, still texting.

"I'm sick of these hoes in this school! Bitch niggas ain't got nothin' better to do besides fuck with me on some lil' kid's shit."

Her statement got my full attention and I put my pager in my pocket to get the full story.

"What happened?" I asked curiously.

She looked at me, and I saw pain beneath the anger, meaning someone had said or done something to get under her skin.

"I was in history class kickin' it with Felicia and Fatima, tellin' them 'bout my weekend and shit, then Bernard's bitch-ass had to open his mouth," she said a heated tone.

My clique was small, especially when it came to females, but Felicia and Fatima were twins who were apart of the family I'd built. They'd come to the states about five years ago from Ethiopia, and even though D.C. was a melting pot of cultures and ethnic backgrounds, they were still treated like outsiders by most. Everybody I fucked with had one thing in common— they were all underdogs in the eyes of the masses, and they didn't give a fuck.

"What did Bernard say?" I asked.

"He started talkin' about his weekend and how he had some freak hoe in the hotel running a train on her."

"OK?" I asked confused, but having a bad feeling just the same.

"He was talking about my mom," she said quietly, her eyes tearing up.

29

Bernard was a part-time dope boy selling a little crack and heroin for his big brother Q. He was really a nobody who thought he was somebody, 20 years old and still a senior in high school, and even worse, he was a bully.

I knew all too well what it was like to have a mother who was a junky, and the embarrassment that came along with it.

Teshia's mom had been strung out on heroin for a long time now, and like any addict there were no limits to what she would do to get her fix.

Teshia inherited her mother's body, which meant the dealers who knew her, would trick with her mom as a way of fulfilling some type of sick, twisted fantasy. I hated it for her, but at the same time, I was thankful I didn't have to deal with the same things because my mom was down south somewhere. I knew my words were useless, so I just pulled her towards me and let her cry like any real friend would.

"I wish she would just stop!" She sobbed into my sweatshirt.

I know that feeling too, just as much as I did the disappointment when the reality set in that I couldn't make it happen. I was still holding her when I saw Bernard's short, bowlegged ass walking towards his all black Crown Victoria. I knew he couldn't see us inside my car and I suddenly got an idea about how to get even with his triflin' ass once and for all.

"Hand me that pistol out of the glove box," I told her, handing her the car key so she could unlock it.

She did as I asked and passed me the all black rugger .380, once she'd taken it out. Zo had given it to me for protection. I checked to make sure it was loaded, flipped off the safety, and chambered a round into the head.

"Mac, what are you gonna do?" she asked. Worry had taken the place of the sadness that had just been in her eyes only moments ago.

"I'm just gonna scare him," I said, as I started the car and followed him out of the parking lot.

I knew the decision I was about to make was reckless, but nobody fucked with my family and got away with it. Once we were a few blocks away from the school I noticed he was headed for Simple City, and for what I had in mind, it wouldn't be a good idea to do it on his territory.

Pulling up next to him at a light, I lowered my window just enough to stick my hand out, and waited on the light to turn green. When it did, I stuck the gun out of the window and pulled the trigger as fast as I could, shattering the late morning calm as easily as I did his passenger side window.

He hit the gas, trying his best to outrun my shots, and I whipped my car up an alley just as quickly, trying to get the fuck out of dodge.

"Bitch, you crazy!" Teshia yelled, laughing hysterically, pure excitement written all over her face.

I could bask in the glow of my victory later, but right now I had to focus on hittin' these back alleys and side streets before the cops responded. I passed the gun back to her and she put it away.

"Yo, what made you do some wild shit like that?" she asked.

"Sometimes words aren't enough, sometimes these pussy niggas gotta know you'll fight back, and not just let them step on you. Feel me?" I asked, runnin' some street knowledge down to my girl.

"Yeah, thanks for havin' my back, Mac. I hope you know I always got you the same way," she replied earnestly.

"I know," I told her, shooting out of the alley and hanging a left on K St., heading up town.

It looked as though school would be cancelled for us for the day, just in case the nigga went to the police about gettin' shot at. The code of the streets wasn't applicable to everyone in them.

"Where we goin'?" she asked, obviously noticing we were headed to the rich side of town which was Northwest D.C.

"I gotta meet up with Success about Jessica's party," I informed her.

"Success, the pimp?" she asked, curiosity lacing her words.

"Calm down and keep your panties on, Slim, this is business and I don't need you starting no damn drama that'll have KP actin' a fool," I quickly said.

"I wouldn't do that, you know I love KP more than anything in the world. I was just curious about Success, I mean, you hear his name in the streets but you don't really see him," she said, taking what she needed from the glove box to roll a blunt.

"Well, you'll see him in a minute, but like I said, I'm on some business right now for my baby's party," I told her checking my mirror for any sign of the cops, or Bernard. If he knew what was smart he'd stay away from my crew, and keep his mouth shut, because he didn't want these kinda problems with Zo. Teshia was like a sister to Zo, which meant he'd act a fool about her.

"Where are you meetin' Success," she asked, before passing me the blunt to light.

"He got hoes workin' out of the Double Tree and the Hyatt right now, so I'ma meet him in between the two hotels," I replied, lighting the spelt and scanning the streets for his ride.

I'd originally heard about Success from my older brother who'd done a bid with him in Tennessee, and then one day he'd blown through the city. The nigga was smart, and good looking, which made him dangerous, but by the time most chicks figured that out, it was too late and he was 'Daddy'. I couldn't knock the hustle though, sex had been selling since the beginning of time and it would never go out of style, why not capitalize?

I spotted his all white 5500 Benz sitting on a one way street, a block down from the Hyatt Hotel, and I pulled up beside him. There was a bad ass, blonde white girl behind the wheel and an equally beautiful exotic brunette sitting next to her. I hit the blunt again and passed it back to Teshia, before lowering my window. I waited as his window slid down and his profile came into view, with yet another gorgeous woman sitting beside him, that one looked Brazilian.

"Say hoe, your eyes need to be where your hands are, on 10 and 2," he said, addressing the driver who had turned her enchanting blue green eyes on me.

"Maybe she sees something she likes," I said teasing him.

"That hoe knows the rules, if you ain't payin' then she ain't playin'. My hoes don't make me dinner they make me rich, dig me?"

"I hear you fam, so let's handle this business," I said, getting back to the matter at hand.

"What's the play?" he asked, as the woman sitting beside him brushed his hair.

I almost laughed, but I knew love could make you do some strange shit for your man.

"I'm throwin' a private party tomorrow night for my girl's birthday, and I want some of yo' baddest bitches there to turn up."

"Where?" he asked.

"At the Hyatt," I answered. That should make it easier on everybody."

"How many girls, and for how many hours?" he asked, getting to the money part of it.

"I want two to dance, and three to spend the night with me and her," I replied, referring to my girl, Jessica.

"Damn! Y'all gonna get down ain't you?" Teshia said, laughing.

I noticed his eyes skate past me and take her in, and the sharp intake of her breath told me just how powerful an effect that one look had on. When he smiled and I saw his startling white veneers with a single diamond in the middle of each tooth, I knew my girl would be lost if I ever let her near him.

"She's family, my nigga," I told him, hoping he'd get the hint.

"We all family, my hoes don't lose when they choose, ain't that right?" he looked to them and asked.

"Yes, Daddy," they all said in unison. The women's chorus didn't help my cause any because I could still hear this bitch, Teisha, breathing heavily in my ear.

"Whatever. How much is all this gonna run me?" I asked, directing the conversation back to the matter at hand.

"Since we family, I'ma do it for five grand, but my hoes don't move without the money first," he answered straight-up and to the point.

"Not a problem. I'll hit you up with the room numbers, and we can meet up to square the bill before show time. How's 9pm?" I asked.

"That works for me," he replied, "any preferences?"

"Yea, make sure the one behind the wheel is in attendance to spend the night," I said, checking to see if she'd look at me again, despite his instructions.

She didn't dare turn her head toward me, but the faint movement of her shoulders told me it took a lot of effort on her part. His next statement let us all know he'd seen it too.

"Hoe, I dare you to look at her," he said in a tone that really meant *try me.* You'll be back on the track before the 'D' in Daddy can pass your lips," he added without blinking an eye.

I laughed at that, wondering if I had what it took to pimp because I could never be a hoe.

"Damn, you hard on 'em, Success," I said, as if I really cared.

"Only when need be, baby girl. Every hoe in my stable needs to know they can be replaced by the next, 'cause at the end of the day, what woman don't want Success in they life?" he asked, smirking at his own humor.

A Savage Love

"Mmmhmm," Teshia mumbled beside me.

Before I could respond my two-way went off and a message popped up. It was Zo letting me know I needed to answer my damn phone. I reached in the backseat for my backpack and searched it 'til I found my cell phone. I knew I would get cussed out for not answering the first time. I know he trusted me, but it still pissed him off whenever I didn't answer my phone, and I understood because I knew it worried him.

"I'll hit you up later, Success," I said.

"Cool," he replied, sliding his window back up, as his car started and eased off into traffic.

"What's wrong, Mac?" Teshia asked.

"I missed Zo's call," I said, agitated at the lecture I knew would come once he reached me.

"Oh," she replied nonchalantly. She'd heard our arguments before, so she knew how ugly it could get over the littlest things.

The ringing of my phone caused my heart to start racing, but I didn't hesitate to answer it.

"Hey, baby!" I said in the receiver.

"Where are you?" he asked, attitude evident with each word spoken.

"I just finished up my meeting with Success about Jessica's party. Why? What's wrong?"

"Did you just get into some shit with that nigga Bernard?" he asked, revealing the real reason behind the call.

Damn, I'd heard of word traveling fast, but it wasn't no damn way my man should've got the news that quick! I opened my mouth to lie, but everything in me told me that would be the exact wrong move for me to make. Zo believed if you lied about something small then you'd lie about something big, so the truth was all I had.

"Baby, I can explain. He…"

"No you can't fuckin' explain because it was some dumb ass shit! Furthermore, we not about to have this convo over the phone right now! Get your ass to the house and wait on my instructions," he said, without another word.

The dial tone in my ear told me whatever response I was gonna give was useless. I didn't say shit. I tossed the phone back in my bag and put the car in reverse, to back up down the one-way street.

"You okay?" Teshia asked, attempting to pass the blunt back to me.

I shook my head no, not trusting my voice. I tried to see through the tears clouding my vision, as I headed towards my house. I hated Zo to be upset with me because it felt like I had let him down like so many other people in his life had done. I never, ever wanted to do that. I never wanted to disappoint him or make him feel as though there was another woman somewhere out there better than me.

"He'll listen to you when he calms down, Mac, you know how he is."

My response was to turn my music on because as much as I loved Teshia, I really didn't wanna hear her voice right now. I wasn't blaming her for what happened. I mean, after all, it was my decision to shoot at the nigga. For real, I was mad at myself because I knew better than to make stupid impulsive decisions, and I should've known word would get back to Zo. I was protected in these streets, which meant when the heat was coming he'd be the first to know.

I took Teshia back to school so she could get her car, told her I'd see her and KP later that night, and drove the rest of the way home in a daze. I didn't wanna sit on the phone and argue with Zo all night, but it was inevitable I'd be getting a tongue lashing. My only solace was he'd be getting out soon, which meant I wouldn't have to hear it as much during our next visit.

After parking the car, I popped the trunk and hopped out with my backpack in hand. There was ten, one hundred dollar bills and a pound of weed in my trunk, which I put in my backpack before heading upstairs to my apartment. My plan was to lie around and get faded until Zo called, or Jessica came home from work.

Opening the door, I stopped to take my shoes off and tossed my backpack on the couch, but a bitch wasn't stupid so I made sure to lock up tight before moving on into the apartment. I rounded the corner to go in the kitchen and his backhand slap lifted me off my feet. All my senses went haywire at once because I could taste the blood in my mouth, from my busted lip. My ears were ringing, and I was beginning to see stars. My mind was screaming *run,* but behind the stars loomed a face I was all too familiar with, despite the anger in his eyes.

"Baby," I whispered breathlessly.

"Baby, my ass, what the fuck is wrong with you, Makayla?

"You shootin' at niggas in broad daylight now?"

I wanted to answer, but seeing him standing in front of me hadn't worn off yet.

"Bitch, get up!" he ordered, as he pulled me to my feet by my hair.

I didn't resist, but I knew I better talk if I didn't want my ass whooped.

"Baby, please, listen for a second! Please!"

"Talk, Makayla."

I quickly poured out the story of what happened between Brenard and Teshia. As he finally began listening to what I had to say, his eyes softened, and I could feel his grip loosening. I knew he understood just how much shit like this affected us both. Once I'd laid it all out for him, I just stood there in front of him, staring intently into his smoldering brown eyes.

"I understand why you were upset, babe, but you can't be doin' shit like that if you expect me to stay out. I just came home

37

today, and niggas already blowin' my phone up, talking 'bout Q's little brother."

"Baby, I didn't know you were comin' home today, you..."

"It don't matter, Slim. You makin' enemies we don't need, and you fuckin' up money 'cause Q is a business man."

I knew he was right, and despite the fact he'd hit me, I was beyond happy to finally have my Zo home with me. What we needed in this moment was to put our mind on other things.

Without taking my eyes off of his, I slowly reached for the belt buckle on his jeans, unfastened it, and unbuttoned them. He didn't say a word, but I could see a small hint of a slow building fire as it burned in his eyes. I pushed his jeans and boxers to his feet and kneeled in front of him. Taking his dick in my hand, and stroking it slowly, his breathing told me I was doing the right thing.

Once I had him as hard as I wanted him, I wrapped my lips around the head of his dick and sucked lightly, but tightly. His moan started deep in his throat and grew into a growl by the time it passed his lips, letting me know I had him open. Slowly, I took more of him inside my mouth, relaxing my throat muscles, giving him a snug fit until I couldn't take anymore. I knew what my man liked and I was gonna give it to him.

Looking up into his eyes, I took my hands and grabbed his firm ass cheeks, pushing him deeper down my throat, before I pulled back quickly, only to glide down slowly again. I could feel the tremble in his knees and I knew the fight was almost won. I increased my speed and felt my pussy throb in rhythm to his dick in my mouth. I sucked harder, pulling him toward me faster, and I started humming because I knew the vibration drove him crazy.

"Ma-Makayla! Baby, I'm-I'm sorry, I-I-I love you!" he yelled, grabbing my dreads, just as I felt the eruption of his climax hit the back of my throat.

I didn't pull away, but instead swallowed and sucked harder, wanting to taste and savor every drop of my man.

"Damn, baby, you know how to welcome a nigga home," he said, his voice filled with lust.

"Mmmhmm," I replied, still slurping.

"Come on, we've got some catchin' up to do," he said pulling me to my feet and scooping me up in his arms. There was no place that felt safer, or more like home to me, and I knew this was my forever.

Aryanna

CHAPTER FOUR
Real Love

"Baby, you know I'm sorry right?" Zo asked, cuddling closer to me while Mary J. Blige's and Method Man's *You're all I need* played in the background. We'd made love over and over again, changing positions as our shadows on the wall grew, and day prepared for night's takeover.

The feeling of having my love right here beside me was surreal, but the swelling in my cheek was defiantly real, and reminiscent of day's past. I know Zo wouldn't hurt me, and he'd just lost his temper because of how serious the situation was. Deep down he loved me like no one ever had, but I had to find the words to let him know we definitely couldn't go back to the way things were when our relationship was mostly physical. I'd learned what not to say or do to avoid provoking him, I just wanted us to be in a good place and move forward in a positive way with our lives.

"I know your sorry, babe, and I understand I fucked up, but I don't want us to go back to how we use to be," I said sincerely and honestly.

"And we won't, I promise. I just lost it earlier because I don't wanna have to kill a nigga my first day out. That's also why I always stress to you to make good decisions. I'll body a mufucka behind you, Slim, and you know that."

"I do know that, baby. I'm sorry too," I told him, taking his hand in mine, and kissing his fingertips.

He leaned into me and placed the gentlest kisses all over the left side of my face where he'd hit me, whispering promises not to ever do it again.

I know some females would've called me stupid or naïve, but they didn't understand he was just trying to protect me. They couldn't know I'd been to hell and back with this man, we'd defied the odds and stayed together through adversity. And since they couldn't know, fuck their opinion.

"Mmm, baby, as much as I'd like to stay in bed all day and night, I'm starving, and I have business to tend to," he said, kissing me again before going to the bathroom.

Once I heard the shower come on, I got up and went to the kitchen to see what we had that could be whipped up quickly. My findings were depressing, which meant we'd have to go out and eat after our showers.

In the meantime, the organized noise in my mind was begging to be let out, so I tracked down my bag with my diary in it.

Crazy Love:

To know love you have to embrace it, truly embrace the good, bad and sometimes the ugliness that comes with it.

It can fill and complete you from the tips of your toes to the roots of your hair, and still, you would only be getting part of what's there for your consumption. And, yet, it can leave you as empty as something that never existed to begin with. How is that possible?

Why do some loves hurt so good, while others make you feel understood, cherished, and dare I say, whole?

At times I feel like love is nothing more than stolen kisses from an abusive lover, plays to cover the damage that no amount of physical or mental make-up can undo or hide.

Yet, and still, I still want it too reside within me, elevating and uplifting everything that it is to create, we and us.

I want it to be enough to wake me up every morning, but regret going to bed at night.

And, while my expectations are high, I feel as if he has met and surpassed my wildest dreams of what I would hope love could be.

Who is he? The easy answer is that he is me, but the truthful answer is that he is who I hope to be with when forever arrives.

I know it's true because I can feel the pain of his love already with the steady rhythm of our hearts that beat as one, despite the distance that separates us.

Together, I, we, us, will prevail and create a destiny that no one foresaw or believed in, and in the end we will be as we should, joined in unity...

The sound of keys jingling and the lock turning broke my train of thought, but that was OK, because my feelings at this moment were as confused as they were clear. I loved Zo, but sometimes love came with more questions than answers.

"Hey, baby," Jessica said coming through the door.

Mentally I wasn't prepared for what might turn into a situation, but there was no avoiding the facts of what was going on. We both knew this day was coming, we just didn't know it would come this soon.

"Hey, how was your day?" I asked, putting my diary down, and pulling out the weed to roll her a blunt.

"It was long, and I'm tired of cleaning up after nasty mu-fuckas all day," she replied, slumping in the seat next to me.

She worked at the Comfort Inn Hotel not far from our apartment on 6th St., which was good as far as commuting back and forth to work, but bad as far as clientele, because it was the hood spot. At times like this I could've reminded her there were easier ways to make money, but keeping my mouth shut kept the peace.

"Are you running a bath for me?" she asked, accepting the blunt I passed her. She took her eyes off of me and looked towards the bedroom.

There was really no delicate way to go about this, so it was best to be up front with her.

"No. Zo came home today," I blurted out.

"He came home? What? How?" she asked, in a baffled tone.

"He wanted it to be a surprise which is why he didn't tell me he'd gone up for parole early and got approved," I replied somberly, not wanting to sound too excited. I didn't want her to feel as though I was just throwing her away like yesterday's trash, but I needed her to know and understand that *he* was my man, and *I* was his lady.

"I see," she said, with a look of hurt and confusion.

Those two simple words spoke volumes and carried a lot more meaning than just their face value. I could see the uncertainty in her eyes. I wasn't sure what I could, or should, say to erase it, and giving her false hope wasn't fair to either of us. But, I did love her, this I knew with as much certainty as I had when it came to my feelings for Zo.

"It's been a long day on my end too," I told her, lighting my own blunt, trying to hide the shaking in my hands.

"I bet," she mumbled under her breath. Her eyes took in my naked body and she could probably smell the sex on my skin.

I chose to ignore the slick comment, and instead, fill her in on the drama from this morning, but, of course, leaving out the plans for her party.

She listened in silence, occasionally shaking her head at parts of my narrative, still smoking and blowing smoke rings toward the ceiling. I could feel her emotionally withdrawing from me and it hurt me more than I'd thought possible. Zo was my dude, but Jessica was my best friend, and had been since I'd met her at D.C. Live more than a year and a half ago.

Despite my dislike for clubs that weren't strictly go-go I'd gone to D.C. Live on a Friday night and met her through mutual friends. Most of her friends were guys, but from the beginning, I sensed something inside her that drew me to her. What started out as casual conversation, ended with us in the back of her Ford Explorer tasting one another. Until this day, I still hadn't tasted a pussy so sweet. It was impossible to spend almost every day with someone and not love them, but my heart belonged to Lorenzo Thompson.

"Jessica, you know I love you," I said, trying to ensure her that what we had was real.

"Yeah, I know, and I know you've been waiting for him to come home for a long time. It's cool," she said, trying to lighten the mood.

I knew she was hurt, and knowing I was the cause, also hurt me. In a way, I was just as conflicted as she was. My intent had never been to cause her any pain, or use her for my own personal pleasures while Zo was away. But, we both knew the time would come, but I guess neither of us was prepared for the moment it finally came.

"Don't do that, Jess, don't try to blow it off like we're nothing to each other," I said, taking her hand in mine, and lacing our fingers together.

When she looked at me I could see the tears in her eyes, and I know they mirrored my own. I leaned in to kiss her, but she pulled back and snatched her hand from me. Tossing the blunt in the ashtray she turned and grabbed my face in both her hands, studying it intently, and I watched the pain vanish as rage took its place.

"He hit you!" she growled at me, not asking a question, but stating a fact she was sure of.

"Let me explain."

"He-fuckin'-hit-you! There's no explanation, Makayla, and you know it!"

"He was just worried because of what I did with Bernard, but..." Before I could get another word out she cut off.

"Anything after but is bullshit, and I'm not gonna sit here listenin' to you make excuses for that muthafucka!" she yelled. She grabbed her purse off the table, and headed towards the door.

"Jessica, wait!" I cried out, running behind her.

She never paused her stride, and she slammed the door in my face. The pain of her walking out on me hurt more than Zo's slap to the face. I hoped she would come back, but deep down I knew that wouldn't happen as long as Zo was here. When I heard him approaching from behind me, I wiped away the wetness on my cheeks.

"What was all that yellin' about, babe?" he asked wrapping his arms around me.

"Nothin', just Jessica being dramatic because she knows what your bein' home means for her and I. It's OK," I said, forcing the sound of calmness in my voice. With each word, I could feel something crumbling inside.

"She'll be okay," he said, as he bent down and kiss my neck.

Taking a deep breath, I composed my thoughts and feelings to the best of my ability, but when I turned around I was hit with another surprise.

"Why are you in my purse?" I asked in an offensive tone.

"Calm down, Slim, I'm just looking for your car keys."

"My keys? For what?" I questioned a second time.

"'Cause I got moves to make and shit to do, I told you that already."

"Oh, well let me hop in the shower real quick before we head out," I said, assuming he'd meant we were going together.

"We? Whatchu mean, we? We didn't conduct business in the streets together."

"But, I've been handling shit while you were gone, so..."

"So, now I'm home," he said interrupting me, "and I can handle my own. Just relax," he replied, after finding the keys he'd been for.

"Relax? Baby, you just came home, which means we should be curled up in the bed together, ordering room service or fuckin' my headboard up."

"Sweetheart that sounds like a good time, and your pussy is the best, but that ain't gonna pay our bills and get us out this dump."

"But baby..."

"Yo, what the fuck are we arguin' about?" he asked, as if my suggestion was the craziest thing he'd heard. "I just lost two years of my life, and it's time to make up for that. All that tender-dick shit you talkin' 'bout can wait, I'm 'bout my money first, and foremost," he said with finality.

He moved past me towards the front door, and I knew it was best to just chill and let him handle his business. Fighting with him was useless when his mind was made up, but knowing what was best didn't always mean you did it.

"You act like money is all that matters in the world! Ain't no money or them niggas you in a hurry to get to hold your mu-fuckin' ass down for two years! I did that shit!" I yelled out before I could stop myself.

My words froze him in place, and I probably should've stopped, but the flood gate was open now.

"Ain't shit in them streets for you, my nigga, and you can't get back what you lost two years ago! You keep fuckin' around and you gonna lose what you got, so you need to appreciate..."

"Appreciate what?" he asked, picking me up by my throat, and bringing me to his eye level. "Appreciate what? And where you gonna go? I own this fuckin' city!" he yelled, as drops of his spit sprayed my face.

"App-appreciate your freedom," I managed to croak out, despite his powerful grip shutting off my air supply.

"I'ma show you how much I appreciate it," he said throwing me on the couch, before walking out of the door.

I continued laying there on the couch, gasping for breath and coughing. I rubbed my hands where his had just squeezed me in anger. I didn't know why I'd kept running my mouth. The last thing I wanted to do was push my baby away from me, especially after not having him for so long. I needed him. I laid there for hours crying endless waves of salty tears. My mind wander and wonder where he was, as dusk gave way to night. I wanted to rewind time just a little, so we could start his homecoming over with a clean slate of celebration, but I knew that was impossible. All I could do now was wait.

Picking up my open diary and the rest of my weed, I finally summoned the strength to make it to my bedroom. Never had my sheets seemed so cold, or the night so lonely. I twisted a blunt, and sat it on my nightstand, as I reached for my pen.

From the Heart:

How quickly tears of joy become surpassed songs, making me wonder if all along my dreams for tomorrow had been mere fool's gold.

My heart wants to hold onto the dream while my mind screams at me to stop being foolish, and put away those childish things. To see what his actions mean instead of being blinded by the bling of his word play.

His words may paint a beautiful picture, but the mixture of truth to lie takes away from the shine, and causes this dream home I've built of happily ever after in my mind to become nothing more than a shrine and burial place.

So are the tears on my face now products of me facing reality and shattering whatever illusions I had about him and I sharing time and space?

If I accept that then I'd be admitting I've wasted time on building us that wasn't meant to be, and that's not something I can believe.

No being is perfect. In fact, it's the imperfection that makes him sexy to me, because God created Eve from Adam to stop that from happening.

Is he my rib? How do I know unless I live and endure the trials set before us?

Only one person knows what's in store for our future, and so, I must lean on His understanding before tumbling down the rabbit hole of my own logic.

I shouldn't try to stop it because what is meant to be will eventually reveal itself. I just pray when it's shown to him he sees that I'm worth more than material wealth.

Aryanna

CHAPTER FIVE
A Change is Gonna Come

The pain in my chest was a steady ache. It had been two days since I'd seen or spoken to Zo and I kind of getting used to it. I knew he was just punishing me for whatever slight I was guilty of, but it still hurt not to have him here.

I'd lost track of how many times and different ways the scene of his release had run through my mind, but never had I pictured it like this. I didn't understand how we could spend so much time apart, and then, because of his selfishness, spend more time apart! *Who does shit like this to a woman they claim to love?* The thought and question had been running through my mind like a monolog on a loop, since he'd walked out the door without a backward glance.

Added to that, was the fact I hadn't heard shit from Jessica, and I had no idea how she'd spent her birthday or where she was spending her nights. At this point, I missed her more than I missed Zo because I was used to him being gone, but not her.

All this bullshit had me in a funk and feeling some type of way, plus, I was funky from laying around smoking blunt after blunt for the last 48 hrs.

One thing I was absolutely sure of was that I couldn't keep letting everyone around me live and enjoy their lives while I was miserable. The game didn't go like that. I reached for my two-way laying on my nightstand and sent Zo a message to bring my mufuckin' car back immediately! He'd been ignoring all my messages, but he was smart enough to know he better bring me my shit.

A hot bath was needed to improve my mood. I dragged my ass out of bed and made the necessary preparations of a soothing bath with salts, bubbles, hot water and mood music. Ordinarily, I would listen to love songs, but I had to get my swagga back in a hurry. Monica's *Just One of Those Days* seemed fitting.

It was becoming painfully evident to me that planning my life around Zo acting a certain way was a flaw, so, it was time to make sure I could take care of self for better or worse.

I spent an hour soaking in the tub, planning the day ahead and the moves that had to be made.

I knew my uncle was probably worried since I hadn't come back through with his cash yet, so it was a must I go see him. I also needed to scoop Teshia up too because I hadn't communicated with her since I'd cancelled the meeting I'd scheduled with her and KP.

It was never my intent to shut the world out, but with my heart aching, I felt like my vulnerability was as evident as a pimple on my face. I knew my crew had my back regardless of whatever, some things just needed to be dealt with without prying eyes. Not to mention, the now faded bruise on my cheek warranted a lot of questions I didn't need.

Climbing out of the tub, I went to my closet in search of something to wear. I wasn't really feeling what I had hanging up, and some shopping therapy was definitely needed. If my nigga thought all the material things in life could keep me happy then I was gonna put a dent in his funds real quick.

I grabbed a pair of blue Polo jeans with the matching jean shirt and my Timbs, figuring that going hood chic could never be wrong.

Twenty minutes later, I smelled sweeter than your mama's apple pie, and looking twice as good with my hair thrown up in a high ponytail, with just a bare dab of makeup adorning my face.

Today was gonna be a good day because there was no more drama on the menu. I grabbed my two-way with the intent of texting Teshia to meet me outside the school, but to my surprise, there was a message back from Zo.

My heart beat hard in anticipation of what he would say and how he would come at me. Was I wrong for expecting him to apologize? After all, I hadn't done shit to cause all that happened. My love for him should never have caused such an ugly response.

Taking a deep breath, I opened his message and prepared to take the first steps towards making up. I read the message once and then again, hoping his short response would somehow become longer, and more words would materialize out of thin air. All he replied back was my car was where I left it with the keys under the mat, and he'd found a ride. No *I love you babe* or *I'm sorry,* just some generic ass message like I was some random bitch he dealt with off the street.

"He got me fucked up!" I said aloud to myself.

I hit Teshia up and told her to meet me outside of the school in twenty minutes. I grabbed everything I needed, threw it inside my purse, and left my apartment with pure determination in my step.

It was a beautiful day outside, with only a slight breeze, and the block was already jumping. D.C. was like NY in the aspect that the city never slept. There was always some shit going down on the streets or in the back alleys, but that's why only the realest survived.

Hopping in my car, I lowered all the windows and opened the sunroof, knowing I'd be hard to miss, and therefore, Zo would know I was doing me. As soon as I started the car up I scanned through my CDs until I came to *Hard Knock Life* Vol. 2 by Jay Z, the coming of age sequel was how I was feeling. It was time for me to get out there and get to the money *myself.*

I turned up the anthem 'til my license plate was rattling along with my rearview mirror, then I pulled off. I moved through the city quickly, flashing my sexy smile at the dope boys holding the corners down, as they hollered at me to pull over for a minute.

Aryanna

Breezing into the school parking lot, I found Teshia, Fatmina and Felicia, all hot boxin' Felicia's run down Bonneville.

When I pulled up next to them they all opened their doors simultaneously—it looked like the inside of the car was on fire from the way all the smoke rolled out.

"Damn, y'all just gonna burn like that right here in the school parking lot?" I asked, shaking my head, laughing.

"That's these two bitches fault," Teisha said, pointing at Fatima and Felicia, "they said if we weren't gonna be in school neither were they," she added, as she slid into the front passenger seat.

"Damn right," Fatima said.

I loved and respected the way my girls had my back, even if I didn't need it. I turned my smile on the twins and Teshia, letting them know their love was appreciated.

Once everyone was loaded up I pulled off quickly, weaving through light traffic. For a while we all kicked it, but all too soon I felt the strain in our conversations, and the elephant emerge in the car.

"So what's up, Mac? Teshia asked, turning my radio completely down. I could ask her what she meant, but that would be an insult to everyone in the car."

"We just had a fight, no big deal, I replied calmly."

"Did you fight or break up?" Felicia asked hesitantly. The question made me feel like there was something I wasn't seeing about this situation. Something had happened and they were trying to tell me without really coming right out with it.

"We fought why? What's going on?" I asked in anticipation

"So, you don't know about Zo's coming home party?" Teshia asked, with empathetic pain clouding her eyes.

"What party?" I asked. The feeling of dread immediately unsettled my stomach like a spoiled meal.

54

"Success threw him a welcome home party last night, and from what I heard, he wasn't acting like he had a girl," Fatamina said in a matter of fact tone.

I already knew Fatamia had no love for Zo, nor did Felicia. *Would they really go so far as to make shit up in order for us not to be together?* I wonder.

"Zo don't even like parties, he begged me not to throw one for his release," I replied, not feeling a bit of the calm I was trying to project.

At first no one replied to what I'd said, but a quick glance in the rearview mirror revealed all eyes on Teshia. I cut my gaze her way and noticed how her skin was taking on a red hue, obvious of her keeping a major secret.

"Spill it, bitch," I said.

"Well... KP and I were invited to a party by some of his friends, but I didn't realize who the party was for or who was throwing the party until I got there," she replied.

"And who was there?" I heard my voice murmur from what seemed like a great distance away.

"Success was throwing the party and Zo was there and..."

"And what?" I asked, almost shouting.

"And, um, um, it was a sex party," she finally managed to say.

The buzzing in my ears started suddenly and I could see her lips moving, but her words didn't come with sound.

"Back up and start over," I replied, pulling into an alley to give her my full attention.

"Okay, he threw a sex party to celebrate Zo's return, and he had a bunch of female entertainment."

"Okay, and?"

"And them bitches was dancin' all up on your man, and he didn't seem to mind! And before you ask, I did try to call you but you ain't been respondin' to nobody's calls or pages," she added in her defense.

I knew she was right about that, but that didn't calm the boiling anger I felt rising within me.

"What else happened?" I inquired, wanting to know more.

"All I know is he disappeared with two bitches into a back room, and I didn't see any of them no more. Once I finished with Success I..."

"Oh so you were so worried 'bout me that you had to jump up and down on the nigga's dick that disrespected me by bringing those hoes around?" I asked, accusingly.

"It ain't even like that, Mac, I..."

"Whatever bitch, save your excuses before they get your ass whooped," I told her, jerking my car back into traffic, causing several angry drivers to blare their horns.

I couldn't even stand to hear her voice at the moment, so I crank the music back up and sped through the city. Within minutes, I was pulling to a stop in front of my uncle's corner store.

I hopped out with fire in my eyes, and pain in my heart. My Uncle Joe did more than hustle, he was the heart of the city, and when it came to the absolute truth, I knew his lips would only speak the gospel.

The way I was walking must have spoked volumes which reflected the type of mood I was in, because he instantly shooed away the chick he was talking to once he spotted me.

"Let me holla at you, Unc."

"I already know," he said, leading me around the corner from the front of the store.

"What's the deal?" I asked.

"Well, I don't know how much you heard, but apparently shit got wild at a party last night."

"How wild?" I replied. I already knew as much as what my girls had told me, but I knew Unc would tell me everything and leave nothing out, even if it meant hurting my feelings. So, now, I desperately needed to hear his version.

"There wasn't no videos, but Success gave the same two hoes the day off, and you know that nigga don't like missin' money," he said, making a crucial point.

It felt like my stomach wanted to bottom out, as I thought of the man I loved more than anything fuckin' some nasty hoes. I couldn't lose my composure though; I had to keep my game face on in times like these.

"Anything else I should know?" I asked. I looked away momentarily, hoping to blink back the tears that threatened to fall wanted.

"Nah, baby, just promise you'll try not to lose your cool," he said, knowing how my temper could be.

At his request, I looked at him, so he could see what my eyes could no longer hide. The way he shook his head told me I'd let my mask down, just enough for him to see the crazy I'd inherited from his brother's side of the family.

I left him standing there, without so much as a simple, *good bye*. With all kinds of crazy thoughts racing through my mind, I retraced my steps back to my car. Without a word to anyone I threw the car in drive and smoked the tires, as my car leapt from the curb. I drove on auto pilot for the most part, because in my mind, all I kept hearing was the uncertainty of my own voice telling me, there was no way Zo would cheat on me. Especially not with whores!

The closer we got to my destination, the more I could feel my heart crumbling, hiding under the truth I desperately wanted to believe was a lie. I didn't know how to accept another bitch trying to take my spot, but I knew how to make an example out of the bitch.

Before I knew it, we were in Northwest D.C., driving past Georgetown University. My interest definitely wasn't in attending school though; I was looking for an all-white Benz. I spotted my target two blocks up, but my concentration broke when Teshia tried to pass me her cell phone.

"It's Zo," she said trying to push it at me again. I looked at the phone, looked at her, and pressed on my gas pedal harder to get to my satisfaction.

I rounded the corner of a one-way street with my tires squealing, and slid to a stop inches from Success's bumper. I was out of the car with lightning speed, despite everyone's protests. Before my girls had a chance to jump out and stop the inevitable, I was standing on the driver's side. Slowly, the window began to lower. I didn't know if the green-eyed white girl smiling up at me had been one of the sluts who fucked my man, but either way, I knew the bitch had more than likely ruined a home or two.

Deviously, I smiled back at her, just before firing a swift left jab that, quickly, connected to her cute little nose, squashing it nicely. I loved how the bones crunched beneath my blow, but one hit didn't satisfy me, so I swung again and again. I was so lost in my anger I tried to climb through the window. I wanted the bitch to feel my wrath, my pain, and teach her a lesson about fuckin' other people's man. With each blow, I thought about Zo, as visions of he and her together cloud my judgment.

By now, everything had become a blur of screaming, cussin', and blood. Until finally, I felt myself being pulled off the sobbing hoe, by multiple hands.

"Y'all bitches better let me go!" I yelled, trying to free myself and get back to dishing out my own personal justice.

"Chill!" Fatamin yelled back at me.

"Bitch, if you don't step away from a pimp's hoe I'ma..."

"You gonna what?" Teshia asked, cutting off whatever was about to come out of Success's mouth.

58

To my surprise, she had my gun in her hand, and she cocked the hammer, ready to put a hot one in his ass. I didn't know when she'd managed to grab it, but the grip she had on it said she'd use it without a second thought. Success must've thought so too because he didn't utter another word or take another step towards me.

"Take this," she said, pushing the phone toward me once again.

When Fatamia released my arm, I snatched the phone from Teisha's hand with the intention of giving Zo's triflin' ass piece of my fuckin' mind.

"Fuck you, nigga! Don't call me after you done laid up with them scandalous hoes, call them bitches! I'm done, and you can..."

I stopped in the middle of my tirade when I realized two things. First of all, he wasn't trying to get a word in at all. And secondly, whoever was on the phone sounded like they were crying, which meant it couldn't be Zo.

"Hello? Who is this?" I asked warily.

"Baby, I need you." It was Zo's voice, but the fact that his tone was laced with tears threatened to stop my heart.

"Zo, what's wrong? Baby, talk to me!" I asked.

My tone went from that of a woman scorned to the loving girlfriend I'd always been toward him. Everything I'd just done didn't matter now, and my only concern was finding out if Zo, the man I loved was OK.

"I need your help," he replied, openly crying now.

"Where are you?" I continue questioning him.

"Your aunt's house in the Capers. Louie's dead. I-I-I."

"I'm coming baby," I said simultaneously tossing Fatmina the phone.

I took off running towards my car. All of those angry thoughts had vanished, and my only concern now was getting to my man's side to comfort him.

CHAPTER SIX
All I Need In This Life

I tested the speed of my car, rushing through the green lights and back streets. I also tested its agility by blowing through the red lights while avoiding several collisions. All thoughts of Zo's party had gone out the window, as I tried to process exactly what all of this meant. The girls screamed for me to slow down while I zoomed through the streets, as if I were fleeing for my life.

If he had killed Louie, then he needed to get as far the fuck away from K St. as possible, and quick! For sure, the nigga's who made up Louie's entourage would have his head on a platter, and they wouldn't stop until he was toe-tagged. An eye for an eye was the only way they knew how to play the game, which meant, not even money could fix this shit.

As I crested the hill and cruised back over into Southeast, I had to hit my brakes at the sight of swarming cop cars in Normandy's parking lot. I didn't know why they were posed up at the popular liquor store, but getting pulled over right now would be a costly move. I crept pass them and hung a left by the navy yard, figuring it was a good idea to get a look at the streets before pulling up to my aunt's.

My aunt's house sat at the corner of K St. and 4th, which was known as the Capers all around the city; Capers, a major drug spot was also one of the few areas cops were afraid to travel in.

I followed Jersey Ave. to I St. then to 2nd street. I then made a loop back around K St.

All these streets should've been moving with money and women, not to mention bad ass little kids running around unattended. But, instead, it was deserted like the Westerns waiting on sundown. Shit was defiantly real.

I crept into the alley directly behind my aunt's house, and positioned my car for the fastest getaway possible.

"Alright, all of y'all listen. I don't know what happened, but what I do know is I gotta get Zo the fuck out of here ASAP. Keep your eyes open and the car runnin', and we'll be back in a minute," I ordered, " and, Teshia keep that pistol ready."

Everyone nodded their heads in understanding. I stepped from my ride with a whole lot of nerves which caused my stomach to flip summersaults.

Opening up the back gate, I crossed the yard quickly, and took the stairs two at a time. I didn't get a chance to knock before the back door was opened, revealing my Aunt Doris standing, holding a Moss Burg pump.

Doris was my mom's big sister and she embodied everything the streets of D.C. had to offer, and wore the scars to prove it. I didn't know of anyone tougher then her—if you thought you were bad she'd show your ass differently.

Seeing her short, square frame from a distance you probably would've written her off as just another black woman born into poverty, but one look at her up close would change your mind. To me she had the kindest brown eyes that held many memories from my youth. When you pissed her off those same eyes would turn a midnight-black, and coupled with the two razor scars crisscrossing her face, you knew what the end result would ultimately be.

Standing there in front of her, I understood why Zo was still breathing; she had the look of a hungry lioness licking its chops, not even a gazelle would stand a chance.

"Where?" I asked, stepping in the house.

"The living room baby," she replied, never taking her eyes off the streets behind me.

I made my way through the kitchen, ignoring the roaches fighting for crumbs on the counter. I entered the living room where I found Zo sitting on the couch with his head in his hands. I didn't know if he was asleep or in deep thought, but I didn't have to get any closer to smell the Hennessey pumping out of his pores.

We both knew drinking for him was like lighting dynamite, because once he reached the over the limit point, all he could do was destroy some shit.

"Babe," I whispered, hoping not to startle him.

At first he didn't move, causing me to believe he was asleep. But, then slowly, he pulled his head away from his hands until I was looking into his hollow brown eyes.

I loved this man, so naturally I always worried about him. But, to see him this devastated and broken, caused a fear in me I'd never known possible.

"Babe," he started to say.

I didn't need to hear him speak another word. I knew he needed me, and at that very moment, I wanted to be there for him. I ran to him and pushed my way into his arms. Neither of us spoke or moved. We simply allowed our heartbeats to synchronize, hoping to give one another the strength we needed in a time like this. He was my man, and I was his woman. Everything else was irrelevant now, and nothing mattered except the here and now.

"I'm sorry, Makayla, I'm so sorry," he murmured into my chest. "I'm sorry for everything, babe, especially for not sayin' it sooner. I shoulda brought my stupid ass home, and none of this would be happening right now."

There was a lot I could say, but I saw no need to beat him over the head when he was already down. What was done was done, so there was no point in dwelling on it, not right now anyway.

"What happened, Zo?" I asked, stroking his head as he lay against me.

"Shit just got crazy," he said, reliving the events leading up to now. "I was at a party, but I left around 2am."

"With them hoes?" I question passed through my lips before I could stop them.

"Makayla! Nothin' happened. All they did was dance and drink with me for a while. I swear," he added.

I wanted so bad to give his ass the 3rd degree, but I filed all the questions on the tip of my tongue away.

"What happened when you left?" I asked.

"I went to Lucky's on the corner and got me something to eat to soak up some of the liquor I'd been drinkin', but after I finished eatin', I realized I had nowhere to go. I didn't know if you'd wanna see me. I just went across the street to Normandy's to get me a bottle. Louie was there when I walked in. We spoke, and he asked about you," he went on, filling me in.

I didn't like where this was going even though I knew the ending. I knew Zo, and I knew how defensive he was when it came to me. Add liquor to the equation and the story pretty much told itself.

"Then what?" I asked.

He paused and took a deep breath before continuing on.

"We went and got in his car to talk business, but he kept saying how it would be a better move to let you run shit. The more I sipped, the madder I got. All the while he was talking I was sayin' to myself, who the fuck this nigga think he is to tell me how to conduct *my* damn business, shit," he said, "most street niggas smart enough to know you don't ask another man no shit like that! Then, I asked him why he was comin' at me like that, and campaignin' so hard for you? Unless y'all fuckin' or some shit like that," he finished.

"Babe, I never...," I opened my mouth to say.

"I know you didn't, Mac," he said, finally looking me in the eyes, "I know you didn't. But, the thought of you with another nigga had me so hot, at the time I couldn't see or even think straight! And he just kept going on and on about you," he said, shaking his head. "So, before I knew what was happenin', I pulled my pistol out and told him to shut the fuck up."

"And then what happened?" I asked again, after it seemed as though he could no longer recount the story.

"We struggled when he tried to take the gun from me, and I- I- I shot him in the head," he finished. He said it as though it had all been a bad dream, as if he were reliving a horrible nightmare.

"Who saw you?"

"I-I- I don't know," he answered, deep in thought. "The parking lot was pretty deserted, but I know for sure the cashier at the liquor store saw us leave out together."

"What did you do next?" I inquired for further information.

"I ran," he answered honestly. "I didn't know what else to do, or where else to go. Comin' here was the only thing I could think to do, 'cause hidin' in plain sight would buy me a little time."

"Where's the gun?" I asked, hoping he hadn't panicked and gotten rid of it just yet.

"I still got it. Shit, Mac, I just killed a nigga wit' it. A nigga who was no better, or worse than me, but nevertheless, a nigga who ran the whole Capers area. There's no way I'd be here unarmed."

"Did you wipe the car down?" I asked. I was trying hard to think of everything I could to help cover his tracks.

"Makayla there was no time to do shit else except get the fuck out of dodge!" His voice was shaky, fearful, and at the same time, regretful.

"Calm down, baby, I'm just tryin' to understand how bad shit is," I said, assuring him I was on his side.

"Shit's bad, Slim!" he replied absolute. I ain't worried 'bout his crew 'cause I got my own team, but it's only a matter of time before my prints come back," he rubbed his hands over his head in an agitated manner.

Aryanna

There was no questioning whether or not he had the right to be worried. Even with D.C.'s corruption issues, the fact that we had the highest murder rate in America, meant the world was watching, and that meant the police were coming.

"What address did you parole to?"

"Yo-yo-yours, why?" he stutter the words.

"'Cause," I answered, baffled he hadn't already realized it. Once they connect the dots back to you that's where they're gonna look first. We gotta go, and we gotta go now, Zo!"

"Go where?" He replied as if he were in a no win situation.

"I'll figure that out. Right now, I need to get back to the house as quick as possible, and get everything we need to run."

"Okay," he said adamantly, "well, I guess I'll wait here, it's safer that way."

Logically, I knew he was right, but I wanted him by my side every step of the way. In case this was our last moment, I wanted to be certain we spent it together. "Baby, you should come with me so we can just jet from the spot," I said, taking his hands in mine.

"I feel you, sweetheart, but we don't know what the cops know yet, so it's safer for you to go alone. I promise I'll be here when you get back." He replied as if he were certain.

"You need to hurry back, Makayla. I know I got a lot of re- spect in the neighborhood, but sooner or later them goons gonna start askin' questions," my aunt said, finally making her way into the living room.

Leaving Zo here was harder than it had ever been to leave him when he was in prison. At least in there I knew he was safe. I brought my lips in closer to his, and kissed him with a passion- ate urgency. I needed to give him my strength. But, I also needed to express my love throughout the corners of his mind, to remove all doubt.

66

"I'll be right back," I said scooting off his lap to make my way through the kitchen and back out the door. Once I was outside, my mind started hatching escape plans. I knew we didn't have a moment to waste.

"Where's Zo?" Teisha asked once I hopped behind the wheel and sped off.

"He's good for now, but I need your help," I said rather than ask.

"Anything, you know that," she said meaning it sincerely.

"We gotta go to my house, but first, I need to go see my uncle again and make a power move. I want you to call KP and have him meet us at my spot," I replied giving orders one by one.

"Got it," she replied, and quickly grabbed her phone.

"Felicia and Fatamia, you know the streets talk, and right now, I need to know everything they sayin'. I'ma drop y'all off back at school, and I want you to start pickin' up any seeds dropped about me, or Zo. Then, page me tonight, and give me the run-down on what y'all heard," I said, thinking on my feet.

I always said I was a boss bitch who knew how to handle business, and I needed to prove that to Zo—his life depended on it now, more than ever.

"Kool," Felicia replied for both of them.

I took the back way out of the Capers and went out on S. Capital St., trying to avoid the police at the liquor store. I still made it to my uncle's in ten minutes. I pulled up and signaled him over to my car, trying hard not to let my paranoia run wild.

"What's up, Mac?"

"Unc, I need you, but do it quietly. And I need you to serve my home girl right here when she comes back in thirty minutes."

"The first thing ain't no problem 'cause it's a lot of mufuckas already askin' that question," he said, talking in riddles, but at the same time, telling me what I needed to know. What you need me to serve her?" he asked, pointing toward the backseat.

"I need four of them thangs, but I only got about $60,000 for you right now," I admitted honestly and upfront.

"You want blow?" he asked with evident surprise.

"Yeah, I gotta make money fast. I can't come get it myself though, 'cause I gotta tie up some loose ends, you feel me?" I answered, looking him directly in the eye.

"Baby, what's going on? Are you in trouble? And, if you are, does it have anything to do with Louie?" he asked, straight and to the point.

By far, my uncle was nobody's fool. Although he was willing to help me out, I knew he wasn't feeling this shit one bit. He'd never had a problem with Zo, but he wouldn't appreciate me going down on the count of Zo's bullshit either.

"I can't get into it all right now unc, but I'm good, and you don't need to worry. You taught me the game, remember?" I asked, hoping to ease his mind.

"Yeah, I remember, but what did I always tell you?" he asked, attempting to find out what I'd learned.

"That no matter how good your run is, you always have to pay the lost some day," I answered quoting his exact words.

"Exactly," he replied.

"I ain't forgot, but will you do it for me?" I asked.

The time he took contemplating and weighing out the options seemed to take forever, and it was senseless because we both knew he'd always help me when I needed him to.

"You know I gotchu, but we gotta do shit my way. You have your girl bring me the money, and I'ma supply the product, but it won't be blow," he stated.

"Why not?"

"'Cause there's faster money than that. I'ma have two keys cooked, and the other two gon' be that horse," he said, offering up better than I'd asked of him.

"I don't know shit about heroin, unc."

"You'll learn. For now, all you gotta do is set up shop at a spot I'ma give you in Maryland and collect the money. Can you do that?" he questioned.

"You know I can," I said without a second thought.

"Then say no more, 'cause you wastin' time by just sittin' here," he said.

"I love you, Uncle Joe."

"Love you too, baby," he said back. "I'll text you the address after your people make the pick-up."

I nodded my head before pulling off in the direction of the school. Traffic was getting thicker, but I managed to drop the twins off and get to my house in twenty-five minutes. I sent Teshia to go run the situation down to KP while I grabbed the loot from the stash.

I opened my door to find Jessica sitting on the couch watching TV., but I still blew past her as if she wasn't there.

"We need to talk," I heard her say, following me into the bedroom.

"Not now," I replied, stripping the comforter, sheets and pillows off of my bed, before grabbing two backpacks out of my closet.

"Makayla, I'm serious. It's not okay to let that nigga treat you any kind of way, and then..."

"Hey! I said not now, dammit!"

I moved past her, and grabbed the razor off my nightstand. I then sliced it down the middle from top to bottom. As quickly as I could, I pulled out all the money, and counted it, making two separate piles.

"What are you doing? Makayla, what's happened?" she asked, worry replacing her previous irritation.

"Nothin' happened, me and Zo are just takin' a trip real quick to have some alone time," I lied, sort of.

"Really?" she asked, surprisingly.

"Yeah, don't you think he needs a vacation after doing all that time?" I asked, zipping both bags and pulling out my two-way to tell Teshia to come up.

"Mac, I know you love him, and I've always respected that, but you know you deserve better, baby."

"Don't." I told her, carrying the bag with the $60,000 in it, to answer the insistent knocking at my door. "I'm comin', bitch," I hollered, so she'd stop beatin' my shit down.

Before I could get to the door to open it, I heard the sound of wood splintering, as the door flew open, followed by cops swarming inside. I had just enough time to drop the bag behind the couch before they were on my ass something fierce.

"Where is he?" they screamed, as they began moving off into the back of the apartment.

"Who?" I asked, playing dumb.

"This ain't the time to be playing any games, bitch!" one cop shouted.

"You know exactly *who*," another cop said."

"I don't know shit, but where's your warrant?"

Immediately after asking the question, a piece of paper was shoved in my face. As I scanned it quickly before they snatched it back, to my understanding they were looking for Zo, and he was wanted for murder. What I'd just read didn't come as a surprise. Zo and I both knew sooner or later, they'd be hot on his. I guess neither of us expected them to come so soon. We at least thought, we'd be able to kick a wheel before shit got realer than it already was, but to avail.

"We found something," a cop said, coming out of the back room, with Jessica in handcuffs. It appeared he had found an eighth of a key of pure China White.

"What the fuck is that?" I asked in disbelief. There was no way she would've had that.

"It was underneath the sink, so is it hers or yours?" the mean cop asked.

I looked her square in the eye and I knew beyond the shadow of a doubt it wasn't hers. And, since I knew it wasn't mines there was only one other person it could belong to, Lorenzo. We stared each other eye to eye for a brief moment before shaking our heads almost simultaneously. My mind was made up, and before I could ponder and back out, I spoke up quickly.

"It's mine," I said, confidently.

"Put your hands behind your back," the officer instructed. "Makayla Preston, you're under arrest for felony drug possession, you have the right to remain silent…"

I heard him reading me my rights, but after the first few words, everything else sounded like words being spoken by one of the animated characters on the cartoon, Charlie Brown.

Aryanna

CHAPTER SEVEN
Hard Times

Suicide:

The avenues of pain in my brain are many, so this journey of despair is seemingly never ending.

No one cares.

Not even a penny for my thoughts is offered, and if it were, I probably wouldn't accept. Why?

Because people pretend to care until the next time something of casual interest comes along and tickles their senses.

Friendships seem so senseless in the face of realities truths, and the proof of that is in how easily comfort floods misery.

It's not pity I want, but damn, is it too much to ask for someone to hold me every once in a while, to comfort me with a genuine smile full of love, and not only tolerance?

I'm expected to tolerate or appreciate the scraps from the dinner table of the emotional feast existing in the world around me?

This can't seriously be how my life is to be lived, yet I give all I have only to see no return on the investment.

The hollow "I love yous" that lack actions to match the verbs are testaments to the insincerity that is more or less governed my life since conception.

Makes me wish contraception was used, so the mistake of me wouldn't be here now contemplating the typical "I'm sorry" note before my ending.

As my mind spins, I see it all so clearly now. I never should've been, therefore, the love and peace I long for so dearly is only at the end of one avenue in this maze.

I'm not crazy. I've lived this life in this skin, in this mind alone.

I've been lonely, wishing someone, anyone would come in. But, they didn't and they won't.

People like me die alone, thirsting for just a drop of love's salvation to quench the ailments that are ancient, and long suffering.

Since everyone else has given up, is it somehow cowardly that I've had enough of me?

I can't say I didn't try. Even when I die, it can't be said that I didn't give everything I had to realize the dream.

Sometimes, things just fall short, and sometimes, life really is the bitch she seems.

Rereading my inner most thoughts often gave me hope or at least some clarity on how to deal with life's constant struggles. I didn't get a sense either this time. I actually questioned my sanity at this exact moment. *Was this what rock bottom looked like? Had a month in D.C. jail actually drove me madly insane, or was I on my way there before the handcuffs graced my wrist?* I honestly didn't know, what I did know was that the people I considered family, who I held closest to me, hadn't managed to get me a single message of hope or remembrance.

So, the only clarity I'd gained from it all was that when you're stuck in this type of situation, you finally realize how truly alone you are. The world doesn't stop moving, and your place in it is easy to fill. The mere thought was some depressing shit, which explained why my mind was looking for a way to end my torment. *But, could I sacrifice his life too?* I thought to myself.

As I looked down, and rub my stomach. I thought of all the ways my mother had never put me first. How it had always been men first and then drugs; the combination of both prevented her from being the mom I needed. I never wanted to be like that with my own child, but at this point, I wasn't in a position to be anyone's mother. Admittedly, I should've thought of that before engaging in the action that prompted the jail nurse to say to me, *"Congratulations, you're having a baby."*

But, good dick would give you amnesia along with a list of other irresponsible ailments. For seven straight days, I'd been trying to figure out what the fuck I could possibly offer this child with so much uncertainty in my life at the moment. And for seven days I'd been reduced to tears, wishing my daddy was still alive to make this incredibly difficult decision for me. I couldn't even ask the advice of another woman because I was in solitary, and judging from the conversations the women down here had with themselves, they couldn't offer me a drop of coherent wisdom.

I wasn't just alone, I was *scared* and alone. I knew I'd been locked away down here because the cops were trying to break me, or protect me from being killed once the word got out that it was my baby's daddy who killed Louie. *My baby daddy?* I definitely didn't envision that statement being made in my life at the tender age of 18.

It seemed like only yesterday when I was planning for my graduation, and the love of my life coming home. Now graduation had come and gone without me. I was in jail, and I had no idea where the love of my life was, or who he was with. Bottom line, shit was ugly for a bitch.

"Preston? Makayla Preston, are you down here?" I heard someone yell.

My first attempt at answering yielded exactly nothing except high pitched moans. I couldn't remember when I had last used my voice.

"Here!" I yelled back, as loudly as I could, which equated right above a whisper.

Putting my pen and paper to the side, I scurried off my concrete slab and began beating on my door with the heel of my hand. I didn't know who was looking for me or why, but it felt good to know I existed to someone, somewhere.

My tray slot was opened, and I backed up so I could see what savior awaited me.

"You Preston?" a rough looking woman asked me.

"Yeah," I answered, dryly.

"How long you been down here?" she questioned me a second time.

"A month, a month I think," I replied with uncertainty.

"Stick your hands through the slot so I can handcuff you. You've got a lawyer visit," she said.

I didn't know who this lawyer was or who had retained him, but maybe I could finally get an answer to when I'd be free.

I quickly slid my hands through the opening, and felt the cold steel close around my wrists when she jingled the key in the lock.

"Be quiet and move quickly," she said once the door was opened, and I was in the hallway.

I barely had time to nod my head before she was propelling me down the dimly lit corridor, amidst the deranged screams for oatmeal, and the catcalls for various servings of my vagina.

We came to an elevator at the end of the hall, and once we were on it, she pushed the button for the first floor.

"Do you remember the officer's name who took you to the dungeon?" she inquired.

"No, I've been down there ever since I came in, and except for the nurse comin' to see me, this lawyer is my first visitor," I replied somberly.

"The nurse, are you sick?" she asked in a sympathetic tone.

"No, I'm pregnant," I answered warily.

"Oh hell, girl, I'm guessing its Zo's too, huh?" Her question hit me like an ice cold bucket of water to the face.

"Do I know you?" I asked, stepping back to get a better look at her face. Nothing about her was familiar, and I'm pretty sure I would've remembered her hard eyes, the dimple in her chin, and her linebacker build.

"Nah, you don't know me, but I'm a friend of a friend. Take my advice, if that's Lorenzo's baby you should seriously consider an abortion," she said bluntly.

"Listen bitch, I ain't..."

My words were cut off as she grabbed me by my throat and slammed me up against the elevator wall.

"I said I was a friend of a friend. I didn't say we were fuckin' friends, so watch your fuckin' mouth," she whispered in my ear, licking my ear lobe. Her touch made my flesh crawl.

Thankfully, I didn't have time to respond or wonder how bad shit was gonna get, because the elevator stopped moving and the door slid open.

She released the grip she had on my throat and grabbed my handcuffs, pulling me behind her like a scolded puppy. I was actually thankful for her direction because the blinding daylight made it impossible for me to see my own hand in front of my face. It felt like I'd had my eyes closed for a month, and now the sun was parked in front of the building site.

She led me into a room and pushed me into a chair, before handing me a pair of sunglasses.

"Thanks," I murmured, still blinking against the light.

"Mmhmm. Is there anything down there you want?" she asked me.

"Just my papers, please," I answered respectfully.

Nodding her head, she backed out of the room, and left me alone with my visitor. I made a quick assessment of the middle aged, gray haired, white guy sitting across from me. The tailor made suit and Rolex, which by the way, didn't tick, brought me to one conclusion, money! Dude smelled like money, and when you're a lawyer, money only came from winning.

A cheap wooden table in the windowless room separated us, but we were still close enough that if he farted, I was guaranteed to taste it.

"Miss Preston, you're a very hard woman to find," he said, sizing me up the way most reptilian predators would do their next meal.

I know I looked a hot damn mess. A whore bath in the sink could only clean so much, but this mufucka was still checkin' me out in my tight black and white jumpsuit. I wanted to screw my face up, but disgust wasn't a luxury I could afford at the moment.

"I've been here the whole time," I replied in a neutral tone.

"Yes, you have, but miraculously you were booked and finger printed under the wrong name," he said. "I have no doubt that this was the cops' way of trying to break you, but their failure and tactics allowed for a dismal of all charges against you," he explained on in further detail.

I didn't know whether to kiss this man or get on my knees and thank God. But first I needed him to answer the million-dollar question. "When do I get out?" I asked, hardly able to contain my excitement. I wanted to jump for joy, but had to play it cool just in case it was another ploy against me from the cops.

"They're processing your paperwork now. As soon as it's done, and you change, you can go," he said with finality.

My tears were instantaneous but silent, as they cascaded beneath the glasses covering my eyes, until they fell like rain drops from my chin. I had no words to describe the joy his words had given me. No one knew how close I'd come to trying to meet my daddy at heaven's gate, but I was taking this as a sign of him saying he wasn't ready for me yet.

"Who sent you?" I asked, curious to know who I should thank once I was free.

"I was hired by Joe Preston to use all the influences I had to find and free you. It wasn't easy, but I'll let him explain all that when I deliver you to him," he answered, proudly for a job he knew he'd done well.

"Thank you Mr.?" During all the excitement, I realized I didn't even know this man's name.

"Goldstein," he replied and smiled.

"Thank you, Mr. Goldstein," I said, reaching across shaking his hand.

The door opened behind me, and the same woman who had dragged me up handed me my poems along with my clothes.

"There's a bathroom across the hall," she said, taking the handcuffs off me.

I followed her directions, and quickly changed back into my street clothes. The difference a month made was massive because my shit was hanging all wrong on me, but that was trivial in the big scheme of things. I was about to be freed, which meant I was free to take my life back.

CHAPTER EIGHT
Unbreak my Heart

Thirty long days had seemed more like years, as I stared out the passenger side window of Mr. Goldstein's dark blue Cadillac STS, taking in the city around me.

Everything looked different and new, yet familiar all at the same time. The girls were thicker, the dudes had just a touch more swag, and even the music had a different vibe. The summer had hit us full force, and from the looks of things everyone was living life. Everyone except me, that is.

Despite my best efforts to take in all the sights, sounds and smells, my mind continued to circle around the millions of unanswered questions I had. I understood attorney/client privilege, but I didn't know this man to be asking him what he knew regarding street talk. It didn't really matter though, because I knew who would have the answers for me, and he was posted in his usual spot as we came down half street.

As the car glided to a stop I opened the door, already anticipating the hug I desperately needed from my uncle. The smell of fish that assaulted my nostrils left me leaning out of the car door, puking violently. Fish was one of my favorite things to eat, but at this point, my unborn child was obviously dictating the menu.

"Not in my car!" Mr. Goldstein exclaimed.

I wanted to say something smart, but I chose to stumble from the car as gracefully as morning sickness allowed.

"You okay, sweetheart?" My uncle asked, rushing towards me, allowing me to collapse in his arms.

"I'm fine, Unc, they didn't manage to kill me," I replied, forcing a smile on my face.

"I know that's right. Come on, let's sit down for a second and catch up, 'cause I know you got a lot of questions," he said.

"Too many to ask, just tell me what's goin' on," I responded in anticipation.

"Well, when they popped you, your girl Teshia came and told me right away, but she said somethin' about Jessica not givin' her the money. Of course, I tracked Zo down to let him know what happened. But, after I found out about him and Louie I knew there was nothin' he could do. The streets have been bleedin' ever since you left. The Capers hooked up with them niggas from out of Trinidad and Simple city, and they came gunnin' for your man."

"Is he... Did they?" I asked, unsure if I really wanted to know the answer,

"Nah, Zo has proven himself to be a warrior out here in these streets, but it cost him a lot," my uncle said.

"What you mean?"

"Well, for one, can't nobody make no real money when they constantly dodgin' bullets. Plus, the dope boys can't fuck with you when your activities bring all types of cops to the area. Zo is still wanted for Louie's murder, but he keeps hangin' around the DMV like he can't be caught," he said, shaking his head.

The DMV was D.C., Maryland and Northern Virginia, otherwise known as the metropolitan area. It was home to all of us, and we knew it better than any cop or outsider, but Zo still had to get away from here before his luck ran out.

"Did he help you find me?" I asked, knowing he must've been devastated without me.

"He was lookin', but I told him I'd handle it so he could focus on stayin' alive."

I could sense something in my uncle's tone, but I let it go so he could finish with the updates.

"So where is Zo now?" I asked the inevitable.

"I don't know, baby. You gotta ask Teshia," he replied.

"Teshia? How would she know?" I asked, in an annoyed tone.

"Well, baby, 'cause last I heard, he'd been lookin' after her ever since KP got killed."

"Whoa, hold up. KP's dead? How? Why? Who?" I asked, dumbfounded.

"You know KP was Hoover, knee deep in the war from the jump, he said truthfully."

I shook my head sadly. Another senseless life had been lost. "I can only imagine how Teshia holdin' up right now," I said.

"Yeah it's been tough, and sad to say, there's even more you don't know about," he added.

The look in his eyes was one of love and sympathy, which let me know that whatever he had to say next was really bad.

"Tell me," I said, taking a deep breath.

"No one is safe in a war sweetheart, and because you didn't pop up in the system, the general conscious was that Zo was hidin' you out. Niggas thought flushin' you out would flush him out too, so they went after the twins to get to you," he said, not making eye contact.

"Oh, God," I mumbled, putting my head between my legs to keep the vomit from coming up.

They caught them comin' out of the Icebox one night and kidnapped them. They were raped, beaten, and left for dead in the trunk of an abandoned car off of I-295 right outside of Maryland.

At these words, I could no longer contain the vomit from coming up, right along with the tears I shed for my friends, friends who had to suffer for no reason. I couldn't put into words the anguish that rocked my body, or the guilt that weighed on my heart.

"Are they alive?" I somberly asked.

"Fatimia is, but Felicia lost too much blood before they were found, I'm sorry, baby."

"I've gotta go see her, I gotta..."

"No, baby, she doesn't wanna see you or remember you right now, and if you love her you'll respect that," he said, rubbing my back gently.

Knowing he was right didn't make it hurt any less though.

"I need to find Zo, there has to be some way to end this war," I said, deep in thought.

"I don't know that there is, baby girl, and right now, it's best to keep quiet about you bein' out."

"So what should I do, Uncle Joe?" I asked. I looked at him with tear stained eyes and fresh throw up on my breath.

"The only thing you can do is live. You're gonna be a mother soon, and that means that your life ain't your own no more."

"How did you know I was pregnant?" I asked.

"A friend of a friend," he replied.

I understood the concept of my life not being my own anymore, but Zo was still the father to this child.

"I gotta at least find Zo and tell him," I said, looking to my uncle for understanding.

"I don't know where he is, baby."

"I've got a few ideas, but I don't have my car," I said, thinking aloud.

"You don't have that apartment anymore either. Jessica upgraded you, but I'll let her explain all that," he informed me.

"I need a phone so I can call her," I asked, hoping I could use his.

"I did that once I knew you were gettin' out, and from the looks of things she didn't waste a second."

Following his gaze, I saw a variation of my car pull up to the curb. In a month's time my factory rims had been switched out for some twenty inch spiders, and my shit was sittin' real low. I looked from the car back to my uncle, then back to the car.

"Who do you think went in with me on the lawyer and everything else it took to get you out?" he asked, smiling.

84

She opened the passenger door and the streets rumbled as 2 Pac screamed about thug life. Kissing my uncle, I made my way to the open car door and hopped in. I had barely pulled the door shut before we sped off.

"Damn, bitch, you in a hurry?" I asked, taking in her profile. Dolce and Cabaña shades covered her eyes, but the salty wetness lining her cheeks was plain to see. I reached for her hand which rested on the gear shift, but she jerked away and put both hands on the wheel. Deep down I knew she'd feel some type of way about what I had done, but I'd hoped seeing me alive and well would dissipate some of that anger.

We needed to talk, but I understood I needed to be patient and let her come to me. I spotted the half of a blunt she'd been smoking in the ashtray and went to reach for it until my stomach lurched. Now that I was with child that meant I couldn't smoke no more, and this was a helluva time to quit, considering how bad my nerves were. Instead of grabbing the blunt I turned the music off, hoping to force some casual conversation.

"You look good, Jess," I said.

"I know. You look like shit though," she stated plainly.

"Thanks, I replied sarcastically."

"Your welcome," she answered nonchalantly.

"Whatever. Look, I need to find Teshia so I can find..."

"Nah, what you need to do is sit back and ride," she said in a demanding tone.

"Okay, first of all I don't know who you think..."

"Save all that bullshit you 'bout to kick, Slim, 'cause I ain't wit' it. You wanna be hard headed and not listen to what a real bitch was tryna tell you but you gonna learn," she said.

"Learn what, Jessica? What was I supposed to do differently, say it wasn't mine? Come on, Slim, you know how the game go," I told her heatedly.

"Yeah, I know how it go, but I don't think you do. Just make sure you payin' close attention so you don't miss the door when it kicks shut on all you gave up for that nothin'-ass nigga."

"I've told you, I love..."

"Yeah whatever, hold that thought," she said, pulling over in front of a red brick house.

I hadn't been paying attention while she was driving, but I definitely knew we were no longer in D.C.

"What's this?" I wanted to know, looking at my surroundings.

"This where your man been hidin'," she answered, pointing toward the house.

"How did you know..,"

Before I could finish the question the front door to the house opened. Both Teshia and Zo stepped out on the porch.

"Nice suburban life out here in Maryland, huh?" Jessica asked.

I opened my door, but before I could step out she grabbed my arm and told me to wait. I didn't understand why, until Zo bent down and kissed Teshia thoroughly, leaving no doubt they were both comfortable and familiar with each other. It felt as if someone had stolen all the breath from my lungs with that one kiss.

My mind was still trying to process what my eyes were seeing, but before I could react, the morning calm was shattered by police popping up from everywhere.

There was nowhere for Zo to run, he was caught. Snatching my arm from Jessica I bolted from the car and was right next to him before the cops realized it. Reaching as far back as I could, I slapped him across the face with all my might. The blow caught him off guard, but when he realized who delivered it you would've thought he'd seen a ghost.

"Bitch nigga!" I yelled, spitting in his face to show my disgust with him. As soon as I turned towards Teisha, she was smart enough to get out of my reach.

"Mac, we can explain," she whined pitifully.

"Ain't nothin' to explain 'cause I'm done with both of you bitches! My nigga, you gonna get everything you deserve, and bitch you better find a hole to crawl into, and pray I never find you," I said with vengeance lacing my tone.

I didn't wait for their retorts because their words were meaningless. I retraced my steps determined not to cry, and climbed back in the car.

"Drive," I said.

"Where to?" she asked.

"Wherever, all that shit is the past now, my baby is the future.

Aryanna

CHAPTER NINE
Alone, but Not Lonely

My mind was running as fast as the tears sliding down my face, and I could do nothing to slow either down. I felt so stupid! I'd given Zo everything— mind, body and soul, not to mention I'd put my life on the line for his triflin' ass. And what did I get in return? For a month he didn't know if I was dead or alive, but instead of moving the world to find me, he was laid up with another bitch. To be honest that hurt more than anything, especially considering that other bitch was supposed to be one of my best friends.

Just thinking about how disloyal she'd been after all I'd done for her caused the tears to fall even faster, but she would definitely get hers.

The biggest question in my mind was what would I do now? As scared as I'd been to find out I was pregnant, I always believed Zo and I would raise our baby together. Now the thought of him being my baby's father sickened me, and as if that weren't enough, he was defiantly on his way back to prison for a long time. I was alone, and I didn't know how to face something so real.

"Mac?" Jessica called, knocking on the bedroom door.

I was in no shape to see her or answer the millions of questions she had, but how long could I avoid her in her own house? I didn't wanna hear no fuckin', *"I told you so,"* or she'd get the full extent of my wrath. I didn't wanna be alone either.

I wasn't sure how much more I could take thinking about Zo and Teisha being together. Every time the two of them crossed my mind, all I could envision was him doing to her what he'd done me so many times when we were intimate. I wondered if she had made him feel the way I did, if he caused her to moan and cry out his name the way I did… The thoughts were agonizing, and I knew I had to stop letting it get the best of me. Life had to go on, and it wasn't good for my unborn baby, but, how?

"Mac?" she called again.

"Yea," I finally answered.

She opened the door and came in carrying a tray. When she sat down on the bed next to me, I saw she'd brought me a bowl of soup, some crackers, some Ginger Ale and some orange juice.

"I know you're probably not hungry, but God only knows what the fuck you ate while you were in there. And, you mentioned something about a baby in the car which means you need to take care of your body, now more than ever," she said in a caring tone.

There was so much I wanted to say, but the tears were choking me. I probably still wouldn't be able to express how much her being here meant to me. The truth of the matter was we both knew she didn't owe me shit. This was love, and she was giving it to me, because I needed it.

"Thanks, Jess, I'll eat some in a while," I lied.

"Will you at least drink the orange juice now?" she pleaded.

I nodded my head in the affirmative, and sat up a little, taking the open container she passed my way. I'd never tasted anything so good in all my life, and before I knew it, the bottle was empty.

"Damn, Slim. Did you eat or drink anything while you were in there?" she asked, laughing.

"I'm telling you, the shit they give you in there ain't for human consumption."

"You sure you don't want to eat now?" she asked again.

"Nah, I wanna take a shower first, 'cause I can't even describe to you how nasty I feel right now."

The look in her eyes told me she understood the double meaning in the words. Getting fucked over by two people you trusted would have you questioning your self-worth, but I was determined not to let myself fall down that hole.

"Everything you need is in the bathroom, and I'll have your clothes laid out on the bed," she said, pointing toward the bathroom.

"Thanks again," I said, kissing her on the cheek, before forcing myself out of bed.

I had to get my shit together. So much about the future was uncertain at this point, but the feeling of having Jessica in my corner was indescribable. It gave me hope that one day I'd get past this shit.

I turned the water on as hot as it would go, took off my clothes, and stepped beneath the fire breathing needles that rained down on me. I'd heard niggas talk about washing the jail off them, and now I finally understood what that meant. Standing there, I let the water beat at the memories I was desperate to forget, feeling the tension release in my shoulder a little at a time.

I heard the door open and close, and suddenly, I felt self-conscious. I knew my body looked nothing like it used to, and not simply because I was pregnant, but because of all the weight I'd lost in the last month. I didn't wanna be seen like that, but before the words could leave my mouth, Jessica was pulling the curtain back and stepping in.

"Jess, wait!" I said, turning my back to her.

"Relax, sweetheart, I'm just gonna bathe you," she said.

I still didn't turn around, but when I felt her running the loofah gently across my shoulders I felt myself relax a little. I couldn't remember the last time I'd felt this vulnerable with anyone, but I needed it. As she continued bathing me, tears slipped from beneath my closed eyelids, but not one of them was for what I'd lost. In this moment there was only room for love.

"Turn around baby," she whispered, but still, I hesitated.

"I-I'm not the same, Jess."

"What do you mean?" she asked, not comprehending.

"I mean, I don't look the same. I've lost so much weight and..."

I didn't get to finish my sentence before she grabbed me by the shoulder and spun me around, puling me right up against her, until all I saw were those enchanting gray eyes.

"You're beautiful Makayla." Her words were soft, and just above a whisper. I knew she meant them from her heart and soul.

"No, I'm..."

"Shut up and listen, you're absolutely gorgeous and that's not something a month in hell can change. You ain't never been one of them bitches that doubts themselves, and you ain't about to start now, understand?" she asked, her voice filled with authority.

For the first time in a long time, I actually smiled because I knew she was right. There were enough females out there with body image issues so I didn't need to be one of them. I kissed her softly on the lips before stepping back to allow her to finish with her royal treatment of me.

While she covered every inch of my body in the delicious smelling soap, she never took her eyes away from mine for more than a few seconds. We were having a complete conversation without the complications of words, and it was good enough to have my pussy beating harder than any bass line.

When she was finished washing me, I took the loofah from her hand and gave her the same thorough, yet gentle, bathing, with all the love and tenderness I'd just received.

Once I was finished I turned the water off, took her by the hand and led her still dripping wet body, back into the bedroom.

"Baby, we don't have to, I know you're hurting right now and...," she began.

I silenced her protests with a kiss that told her my hunger was over riding my pain, as I pushed her on the bed and climbed on top of her. I could feel heat radiating from every part of her body that my lips touched, as I worked my way, slowly, from her ears to her neck, on down to her titties. I sucked on her nipples and bit them gently, until her back was arched and she was begging, and only then did I kiss my way lower.

From the first flick of my tongue across her clit, I felt her whole body spasm and her juices gushed into my mouth faster than any waterfall.

"Oh, God suck this pussy, Mac. Please," she begged.

I did just that, making her cum again quickly, which had my own pussy dripping wet.

Before I knew what was happening, she was pulling on me and demanding to taste me, but I wasn't done yet. The easiest solution was to flip around into a 69, but the moment I felt her tongue dive inside me, I knew my concentration was lost.

"Jess, wait, baby w-wait, oh shit!" I cried cumming so hard, my entire body quivered.

She drank from me as I'd just done to her, matching me lick for lick and bite for bite, until all sense of time and reality were lost. Finally, when I couldn't take anymore I curled up in her arms and opened my mind to what I prayed was a peaceful sleep.

Feeling her arms around me gave me a sense of security and safety that I hadn't known in a while. Within minutes, I dozed off. For once my sleep was dreamless, but I didn't mind considering my real life was enough of a nightmare.

I woke up to finding the sun shining, but I had the bed all to myself. On Jessica's pillow was a single red rose with a note telling me to open the card on the nightstand, because it might help put things into perspective. I did as she told me, and what I found was a complete surprise.

Single Mother Poem:

Aryanna

The woman you are is comparable to none, because you have by far exceeded any expectations one could list.

If I was pressed to compare I'd have to insist you were nothing short of an angel though, OK, some sort of super hero that's forever hidden in the shadows.

A lot of people may not understand, but I know just how precious you are and how hard it is to do the job you do.

After all, being a single mom isn't simply something you go through; it's what you give your life to in hopes of making your child's life better.

It's the weathering of offers whether or not the man or men in your life are there to hold your hand.

Is it any wonder that a woman is forever stronger than a man? I see women as beauty's essence physically present, but a mother takes what I thought beauty was to a different level.

Hear me when I tell you, the world would never know good without that guiding love, only as woman and mother gives.

I'm a man, and if I live forever I'll never possess the grace, strength or determination that is shaping the lives of kids around the world.

Boys and girls alike are being given the light of life from God through you, so this praise is long overdue, because your worth should've been recognized.

I heard the lies growing up of "It takes a man to raise a man," but tell me how can that be true when it's through a woman's teachings that my eyes were opened to what a real man is supposed to do?

Mama's baby daddy's maybe is the saying, and the truth in that is plain to see because it was a beautiful single mother who raised me, who made me, who gave me the tools and abilities to appreciate the beauty born of some cowardly man's decision to leave.

So, a single mother is someone I will always salute as proof of what truth means and embodies.

I thank you, I love you, and more importantly, I see you for everything you will always mean to every child who thinks being fatherless is something to pity.

Wiping the tears from my eyes, I had to smile because she'd somehow found the words I needed to hear. It would be easy for a woman to give the message of encouragement to another woman, but the fact that the author of this poem was a man gave me hope in a different way.

It was still too early to tell what my baby was, but I felt it was a little boy, a little boy I was more than capable of raising into a respectable man, with or without his daddy's help. I didn't have all the answers yet on how to accomplish all this, but at least now I knew with some certainty that I was gonna rise to the occasion.

"I see you're finally awake," Jessica said, coming in the room with a plate of fruit and a bottle of orange juice.

"I just woke up. Thank you for the rose and the poem, they're both beautiful, babe."

"Your welcome, I just wanted to do something to make you smile," she said, smiling down at me.

"You did that several times yesterday," I replied smiling.

"You gave as good as you got, that's for damn sure. You need to eat something else though," she said, handing me the plate of fruit.

"I know I'm pregnant, but damn can a bitch get some bacon and eggs at least," I said laughing.

"You sure your stomach can handle all that grease right now? I know the baby will be fine, but you gonna be riding that toilet something serious!" she warned, laughing.

I hadn't thought about the period of adjustment I'd need, and since I didn't relish the thought of being confined to the bathroom, I ate the fruit without argument.

"So," she said looking at me…

"So, what? The baby? Yeah, I found out while I was inside. And, yes, it is Lorenzo's."

"Figured that, what are you gonna do?" she asked.

"What do you mean? I'm having it of course."

"I know that, babe. I mean what are you gonna do as far as Lorenzo goes?"

"I don't know the answer to that right now."

I could tell my answer wasn't the one she wanted, but this decision wasn't about her. At this moment I didn't hate Lorenzo, I just hated I loved him because I knew I deserved better than what he'd given me.

"Let's talk about this house," I said, changing the subject.

"What about it?" she asked me curiously.

"Really?" I said with a smirk on my face.

"I mean, it's ours if you want it to be. I got rid of your apartment in the city and moved out here to Maryland, so we could have a fresh start."

"Okay, but this looked like a big house from outside," I replied.

"Five bedrooms, three and a half bathrooms, and a finished basement; it's got room, but it ain't no mansion or nothin'," she replied nonchalantly.

"For what it would cost, especially considering the location, it's damn near a mansion," I said, opposing.

"How can you afford that?" I wondered, wanting to know.

"I know your uncle told you I never gave Teisha that money. I didn't trust her," she finally admit.

"Okay, that was only $90,000."

"Well, I took that and went to work for your uncle," she said with a huge grin across her face.

"You what?" I asked in disbelief. I knew how she felt about the dope game, so I couldn't see her just waking up one morning and deciding to hustle full time.

"When you went away, he and I both understood it was gonna take some real money to get you out of trouble, big money! So I did what I had to do," she stated simply, causing my heart to melt even more.

"So you-you did it for me?" I asked, feeling my eyes tear up once again.

"I'd do anything for you, and you know that."

What she said actually left me speechless. Here was this beautiful loyal woman that I'd actually been stupid enough to put on the back burner for a nigga that turned out to be a piece of shit. How could I have been so blind before now? Taking her hands I pulled her into me for a kiss, hoping my actions would show the thanks she deserved.

"You gettin' ready to start something, Slim," she warned, caressing my nipples lightly.

"Is that a problem?" I asked, sticking my finger inside myself before bringing it to her lips, for her to suck on and taste me.

Greedily, she licked the juices from my finger, but resisted when I pulled her towards me.

"What is it?" I asked, surprised by her rejection.

"We have to go, I have some business to attend to, and your uncle wants to see you A.S.A.P."

I hid my disappointment behind a smile of understanding, and grabbed my orange juice as I got up to get dressed. Now that I'd made up my mind about my baby, and the ending of my relationship with Zo was official, a sit down with my uncle was needed, so I could put my future together.

After putting on a blue, Polo sweat suit, and my all white shell toed Adidas, I threw my hair in a ponytail and went back in the bedroom to find Jessica standing there with my gun in her hand.

"What are you doin' with that?" I asked, stunned momentarily.

"Givin' it back to you. I've got one in my truck, and I want you to put this back in your car for protection," she said, reassuring me.

"Is there something I need to be worried about?" I asked.

"The fact that Zo killed Louie ain't been forgotten so I'd just prefer you were safe at all times," she simply replied.

What she said made sense, but her eyes still said there was something she was holding back. I took the gun from her and then my car keys, and followed her to the two-car garage.

"What time will you be home?" I asked.

"I shouldn't be more than a couple of hours, but here's a couple grand for you to go shopping after you see your uncle," she said, holding the money out to me. It felt weird to be taking money from her, but I guess at the end of the day, it was my money.

"Be safe out there and I'll call you as soon as I can, here's a cell phone in case you need to call me," she added.

"A'ight, babe, you be safe too," I said back.

As I got behind the wheel of my car I wondered what she wasn't telling me.

CHAPTER TEN
Trust No One

I didn't go straight to the city to see my uncle, because after being imprisoned in a 6 by 9 cell for a month, I wanted to wander around for a bit. Even though I hid behind the tint of my windows, I still enjoyed the sights and sounds of D.C. in the summertime.

There were kids playing in fire hydrants, while the young girls sat on stoops braiding their dudes' hair in between sales. I saw old ladies sitting around gossiping from porch to porch, and it made me want to go see my Aunt Doris, but that didn't seem like a safe decision to make, so I decided against it for now.

I ended up grabbing some chicken wings from the carryout, taking them down to the point where I could eat and watch the world go by.

The children were running around playing while their families cooked on grills. I couldn't help but wonder if that would ever be me and my baby.

Sitting on the hood of my car looking out at the filthy Potomac River, I thought back to how many days I'd wished for more family time. I didn't want to grow up like the Cosby's; I just wished I had more memories of good times than I had. I may have been unable to express it to anyone else, but I missed my daddy more than ever right now. I needed him. He would undoubtedly be pissed at the position I was in, but his anger wouldn't take away from the advice he would give, or the shoulder he would offer me to lean on. He'd always said he had big shoulders, and I could rest my problems there anytime, but at the time, I hadn't realized how much I'd come to need them.

Wiping the tears from my eyes, I actually allowed thoughts of my mother to cross my mind. There was still so much anger and bitterness I felt for her, I tried to keep my mind away from ever thinking about it. What type of woman chooses a drug or any addiction over the life she chose to bring into this world? My child wasn't even here yet, and I still couldn't comprehend a decision like that, but sadly, I was just one of many in that long line of statistics.

I understood society would probably see me as just another poor black girl who would perpetuate the statistic now that I was a pregnant teenager, but I'd never be like my mother. The child I was carrying would know nothing except love and complete devotion, because I'd die before my baby experienced an ounce of the heartache I'd known.

It was time to put some type of plan together, or my words would just be hollow thoughts, and those did my baby no good.

After eating my wings, I hopped back in my car and finally made my way to the corner store, where I found my Uncle Joe sitting out front. In my heart, I knew I was safe with him, but we were still only a hop, skip and a jump from the Capers, so when I got out of the car I had my .380 tucked in my sweat suit pocket.

"You look a lot better then you did yesterday," he said, opening his arms for a hug.

"Thanks, I do feel somewhat better."

"But?" he asked, knowing I had left something out.

"I know you heard about Zo," I stated.

"Yeah, I did. I also heard where they found him at."

"Yeah, but that doesn't change the fact that he's my baby's father, or the fact I still love him."

"Still love him?" he asked in a somewhat baffled tone.

"If I'm being honest, then yeah, I do, but I love me more, and I love this baby growing inside of me more than I love myself."

"That's good, and that answers my question of what your next move was gonna be with regards to my great niece or nephew."

"No question, I'm keeping it." I replied with finality and assurance.

"You gonna tell Zo about the baby?" he inquired.

"What you think I should do?" I asked, seeking his opinion.

Through his silence I could see him giving my question heavy contemplation. I knew from a street prospective, he liked and respected Zo, but blood was thicker than water, so his loyalty would always fall on my side.

"I got no love for how he treated you, and that's something him and I will get to, but I don't see how not telling him is the way to go," he replied.

"I don't know how long he's gonna be gone, but one day my child is gonna ask who their father is. The nigga may not be shit, but I don't want my baby lookin' at me like the bad guy because I kept Zo away," I replied as honestly as I could.

"True," he agreed.

"I'm not ready to see him or talk to him though, so…"

"Say no more. I'll take care of it, but you gotta do something for me," he added.

"What?" I asked warily.

"Leave Jessica alone."

"Excuse me?" I replied, caught completely off guard.

"You heard me. I want you to fall back from her for awhile. And I don't want you to retaliate against Teshia, at least not now," he said.

"Okay, it's obvious you know some shit I don't, so I'ma need you to make sense, because right now you don't," I responded.

"The streets talk, sweetheart, and with you just gettin' out the last thing anyone needs is your name comin' up in connections with anything funny like disappearances or drugs," he said.

What he said made perfect sense because just because the cops had Zo didn't mean they wouldn't be watching me, especially since they actually found dope in my house. The problem I was having was that his eyes said there was more to it than just the logic he'd hit me with.

"What's up, Uncle Joe?" I asked, looking him scare in the eye.

"What do you mean?" he asked.

"You know what I mean, so please don't play me like I'm stupid."

Don't start trippin', Slim, ain't nobody playin' you," he replied defensively.

"Okay, let me try a different approach. Are you still gonna be doing business with Jessica?"

He didn't open his mouth to answer, but the answer was right there in his eyes.

"I'ma take that as a no. So are you gonna stop insultin' my intelligence and tell me what the fuck is goin' on?" I asked in a demanding tone of voice.

"What would you say if I told you Jessica was the one who tipped the cops off on where to find Zo?" There it was. He'd finally put his suspicion on front street. I couldn't believe the accusation he was making, but why would he lie to me. He wouldn't. Would he? Now, my head was really fucked up. I didn't know who was who, or who I should trust.

"I would say you're out of your damn mind! Why would she do that?"

"To have you all to herself," he said, stating the obvious.

"She wouldn't do that, Unc."

"What if I told you she was the only person who knew Zo was laid up with Teshia? And when I tell you that, you're gonna ask how she knew, to which I would say she was the one who found the house for Teshia to move into because Teshia worked for Jessica," he explained, putting the missing pieces together.

"No…"

I wanted to put forth a logical argument, but my mind kept circling around the fact that Jessica had picked me up and taken me to where Zo and Teshia had been, only moments before the cops got there. Nobody had luck like that. *But would she really do something that spiteful knowing how badly it would hurt me?* I was having a hard time wrapping my mind around it, I mean, I knew how much she hated Zo, but... My thoughts faded, and I questioned my uncle a second time.

" Are you sure, unc?"

"Baby girl, you know I don't wanna hurt you, but I need you to be aware of who you fuckin' with. And for that reason, and that reason only, we're gonna take a little ride, as long as you promise to play nice," he said with humor and seriousness together.

"Okay, I promise," I concurred.

"Mac, I'm serious."

"I heard you," I said.

He still looked, more than, a little leery, but he still followed me to my car. As soon as we pulled away from the curb and he started giving directions, I knew where we were going. This nigga was bold to be taking me to her house, but I guess he wanted me to hear it from the horse's mouth.

Within 30 minutes we pulled up out front. He pulled out his phone to call her outside. My hands involuntary clenched around my steering wheel as soon as I saw her, and it took everything within me not to pull the pistol out of my pocket. She gonna get in the backseat and we're gonna talk. Remember, you promised to play nice." He reminded me.

"I didn't say anything. I simply tried not to bite a hole in my damn tongue. I could see the fear in her eyes when she climbed in the seat behind my uncle, and she was right to be scared, but I wanted to hear what she had to say for myself.

"Speak bitch," I ordered.

"Mac, I'm sorry, I'm so sorry."

"Listen, fuck your apologies!" I said, my pitch already rising, "just tell me whatever I'm here to listen to."

"Makayla," my uncle said taking my hand.

"I-I been working for Jessica ever since you went in. She didn't trust me with your money, but she knew KP and I could flat foot the work she was getting from your uncle. Wh-when KP died we kept going, but she said I had to move. One day she came to me and said she'd got me a house. Since nobody knew about it Zo laid low here when things heated up in the streets, and one day Jessica popped up and saw him, that was a week ago," she said nervously.

"How long had you been fuckin' my man?" I asked, as I felt my temperature rising by the second.

"It wasn't like that, Makayla, I swear," she said.

"So you didn't fuck him?" I questioned her.

"It wasn't supposed to happen! You my best friend and..."

"Friend? Friend! Was I your friend when Zo's dick was inside you? Was I your friend when you were swallowin' his cum, you nasty bitch! Get the fuck out my car!" I yelled, unmoved by the crocodile tears I saw from my rearview mirror.

"But, Mac."

She quickly shut up and hopped out when she saw the pistol I pulled out of my pocket. I started the car and headed back to the city, my mind in complete chaos as I tried to process everything I'd been told. My heart hurt so much for different reasons, but each reason was like a knife reaching all the way to my soul. Being blinded by tears made it hard to drive, but I eventually managed to get us back.

When I pulled up to the curb my uncle didn't get out, we just sat there in silence with my pain taking up all the breathing space.

"I know it hurts and I know you're upset, sweetheart, but you gotta start thinkin' about yourself and that baby now. You gotta focus on what's important, you hear me?" he said.

I didn't trust my voice so I simply nodded my head. Reaching into his pocket, he pulled out a wad of money and put it in my hand.

"You stay out of these streets. If you need anything you come to me, but if I hear about you hustlin' I'ma fuck you up my damn self and I ain't playin'. Make sure you go buy a phone or two-way and hit me with your number so I can keep tabs on you," he said in a fatherly way.

"Thanks, unc," I said, wiping my eyes again.

Once he got out of the car I drove around the city, aimlessly, for an hour before heading back to Jessica's house to find the answers I needed. She wasn't there when I got there which gave me time to grab a pen and paper so I could release some of what I was feeling inside.

Friend or Foe:

Friend, to begin with, I detest the word because most that use it put the most absurd meaning behind it.

They find it convenient to misuse it when a need arises that benefit a majority of one, namely self.

Selfish motivation seems to be the one requisite need. When constructing a friendship of grand design, one finds in the idiot's guide of how to build a house of cards.

Illusion is the tool utilized when painting the picture of loyalty, a word that truly defines the bonding of one to another to give a foundation of what's needed.

I've heard the word used so loosely that I find myself wondering what does it all mean. If I love you, are we friends? If I pretend to have your best interest at heart, am I partial to your feelings so long as they benefit me? Is our friendship circle complete?

I'd like to know what makes me a friend because for all intents and purposes the word foe seems to be firmly defined in the aforementioned category.

So, I'm sorry I can't be sorry for not having friends because in the end, I feel I'm saving my own life, or at the very least, taking it into my own hands.

A knife in the back wounds fatally. But, who can I blame for me not seeing the malice in all the smiles given freely? Who do I hold accountable for failing to protect me from me when it's willful ignorance turning the seeing eyes blind?

You're probably asking yourself if I possess an enlightened mind, or am I simply the owner of a cynical soul turned so by times hold on me, and extenuating circumstances.

What if I said my glass was both half full and half empty? Could you understand the clarity with which I glanced at the future a time or two?

I saw sights of meaning unseen by those with their eyes wide shut to all that's possible if one redefines what friendship means.

Dare I dream that loyalty, honor and principle play a part in the grand scheme of things when it comes to uniting in a way outside of the complications imposed by sexuality?

I do dare, but only because today a woman called me friend and I found myself wishing it wasn't a lie. But it had to have been because friends demonstrate with actions, and her actions imply that she still doesn't know why the word she chose is not meant as advertised.

Two lips will say anything, but in the eyes the truth does not hide…

'Babe, are you here?" I heard Jessica call coming through the door.

I didn't respond, but instead I went into the closet and started pulling my clothes out. I may not have been able to fit them now, but I'd be gaining weight in a hurry.

"Mac, where are you?" she called again.

I came out of the closet with my arms full to find her standing in the middle of the bedroom looking at my first pile of clothes.

"What are you doing?" she asked.

"What does it look like?" I snapped.

"Did you buy that many new clothes?" she asked with a nervous laugh.

I rolled my eyes and went to grab some more of my stuff.

"Hey, what's going on with you? Talk to me, babe," she pleaded.

"You wanna talk, cool let's talk," I said. "How did the police know where to find Lorenzo?"

"I-I don't know," she replied, looking every bit like a deer caught in the headlights.

I didn't even entertain her response, but instead I began to shove my clothes in a bag

"Just stop for a minute and talk to me Makayla."

"I tried talkin' to you, but you wanna come at me with bullshit! How 'bout this, I talked to Teshia, does that help?" I blurted.

"Talked to Teshia about what?" she asked, playing stupid.

"Really, Jessica? That's how you wanna play it? I don't need this shit."

"Okay wait," she said, taking the bag from my hand, sitting it on the bed.

She reached for my hand, but I pulled it back and crossed my arms over my chest.

"Tell me what to do, Mac. I love you and I'll do anything for you, you know that," she said.

"All I want is for you to keep shit all the way real with me."

"Okay," she agreed.

"Okay, so did you tell the police where to find Zo?"

The guilt was evident in her eyes, and right behind that was the blind panic. The tears started immediately, but I couldn't find it in myself to feel bad for her.

"Makayla, you know he's a bad guy. He doesn't treat you at all like you deserve to be treated, he just uses you! It was me and your Uncle trying to find you and bring you home, not that mother fucker!"

"But that mufucka is my baby's father, and now because of you, he could be in prison for the rest of his life!"

"That baby is better off without him! You and I can raise it together and give it all the love in the world," she said selfishly.

"First off, who in the fuck are you to decide that my child is better off without his or her father? You're barely an adult your damn self, so try worrying about your own life instead of planning mine!" I shouted.

"Baby, I only did it because I love you, you've gotta see that," she begged.

"You love me so much that you forced me to be a single mother? That's love?" I asked, my tone resonating my anger.

"I promise you're not in this alone. I'll be with you every step of the way," she said.

"You really didn't think this all the way through did you? You're a dope dealer now, *and* you're a snitch! Those two don't mix, so you lucky to be alive right now and my baby don't need to be around that. I need some time to think," I said, grabbing my bags, preparing to leave.

Before I walked out, I looked in her eyes and I could see she finally realized how badly she'd fucked up. Too little too late though.

CHAPTER ELEVEN
New Beginnings

The Key:
Life's mysteries are many, and the hurts seemingly unending, yet somehow your love has made whole in me what was missing.

Sometimes, I can't understand it, like listening to a language foreign to me, but the feeling of living in a world of possibilities made possible simply by your being, is proof that your love is what I wanna lose myself in.

You've opened me in ways I'd forbidden, found the heart hidden, and showed me what it means to be a team of "We."

Lightening striking is the only thing comparable to the force of your love taking me by surprise, giving light and life to these eyes that have seen even darkness' darkest deeds.

You're amazing, making me wonder how could the same God that made you, make me so inadequate by comparison. Maybe I was just made to cherish the evident perfection in you, and appreciate your love being the glue to rebuild what I once thought destroyed.

I don't question why the gift of you is given, I live in the fact that the verb is gone, and we're moving on to what destiny has in store.

To think I knew love before, kind of makes me laugh now, because I'd compare that to the reduce scales that don't exist in reality. Anything previous was childish fantasy built on half-truths, proven by how quickly it all vanished.

The woman I am now is solely a representation of the gift you are, the gift who kissed the scars of my past hurts and gave birth to the queen I'm meant to be.

So I guess what I'm saying is, "Thank You, Thank You for making me, ME!"

June 2000

Twenty-four months later

"Welcome to McDonald's, can I take your order?"

"Yeah, uh, give me the big Mac meal, and super-size it with your phone number," he replied.

"Whatever boy! I'll be out in a few minutes," I told him, taking off my headset and grabbing a bag to put some food in.

"Is that Kill?" my co-worker, Anisha, asked.

"Yeah, that's his crazy ass," I said, laughing.

"I should've known since the only other time you smile that hard is when your son is around," she said.

I stuck my tongue out at her, trying not to blush under her astute observations when it came to how Cameron made me feel. Lorenzo Jr. was far more the man in my life, but I couldn't deny that Cameron "Killa Cam" Austin made a bitch feel some type a way.

When it comes to heart break, the road to recovery is long and rough, especially when you've had a miniature version of that someone to love every day. He looked and acted like his daddy in so many ways from the very moment he was born, I didn't know if I'd ever get past the feelings of heartache and betrayal, but I did.

Or at least, I found a way to make peace with what once was my happily ever after. I focused solely on my son, and being the mother he deserved, which started with eliminating the bullshit around me.

I loved Jessica, but I could never accept her calling the police on Lorenzo. I kept my car and she kept her new house, and that was the end of that.

As much as I'd just wanted to run away and never look back, D.C was still my home and I wanted my son to have that same homegrown feeling. Plus, his father was still on trial for murder, and despite my disgust with the nigga, I knew it wasn't right to keep his child away from him. I wasn't ready to see him yet, but he got pictures of LJ and I made sure to tell my son who his daddy was, Cam was great with him too.

Moving to northeast D.C with my great aunt was how I ended up meeting Cam, even though I'd sworn off dealing with nigga's who were "bout dat life." He was different though, and I knew that simply because I'd met him in the last place the dope boys and misfits kicked it, church.

You could tell a lot about a man based on the way he treated the woman in his life, so for Cam to take his mom and grandma to church on just a regular Sunday service, said a lot. Most niggas could be bothered for special occasions, but Cam did it whenever, just to make them happy.

I'd like to say it was the first thing I noticed about him, but I'd be lying because the negro was fine! I always said I'd never fuck with a dude prettier than me, but this mufucka, right here was too fine to pass up.

Easily six-one, with that light, butter toffee complexion, jade green eyes, and long hair that graced his shoulders like a lion's mane. The way his suit hugged him you could tell his body was a work of art— and the first time I saw him naked, I didn't know whether to pray *to* him or prey *on* him! Saying he was a pretty boy was an understatement, but the intriguing part was he was very humble.

Bitches were falling all over themselves to get at him, but he kept his poise and didn't let it go to his head. He was from Baltimore, and maybe that was them niggas' swag out there, but no matter the reason, I still found his humble side sexy.

The feeling of betrayal allows you to forever move with caution, and so we didn't do anything besides enjoy each other's company for a while. He was a year younger than I was, and a fruit town brim blood, but he carried himself with maturity that surpassed his years. I wasn't too keen on being involved with another gang member, but I decided not to judge a book by its cover, or judge him by my past.

Here we were nine months into our friendship, and I could plainly see he was nothing like Zo. I wasn't into titles, and I was definitely taking it slow, because of my heart as well as my son, but my auntie called us the "married friends". We spent a lot of time together as a family, and he spoiled both of us rotten in all the little ways that's mattered. Also, his business life didn't spill into his life with us, which was really important to me. He was a good man, even if he was a bad boy.

"When you gonna hook me up with one of his friends?" Anisha asked, snapping me back to the here and the now.

"When your ass stops being shy and talkin' shit that you can't back up," I told her, putting chicken nuggets in the bag for LJ.

"I ain't shy," she mumbled, stepping to the counter to take someone's order.

After the fallout with both Jessica and Teshia, I'd sworn off women in all forms, except for my OBGYN, but Anisha had worked her way into my heart. I looked at her like a little sister who hadn't come into her own yet because she was just a 17 year old chubby kid. She didn't see how beautiful she'd look with a little work, or how most dudes didn't see her as chubby, but as thick and juicy. We were about the same complexion, but she had hazel eyes, short brown hair, and stood about two inches taller than me. I told her all the time how cute she was in the face, and even flirted with her when I was drunk, but she still didn't believe me.

"If I set you up on a date for this weekend will you go?" I asked her after I'd clocked out.

"A double date?" She asked with a hopeful expression that made me laugh.

"Yes crazy ass, I wouldn't feed you to the wolves just yet."

"And you're gonna help me get ready?" she replied with excitement in her tone.

"Yes bitch, we'll go shopping and everything! But you know we ballin' on a McDonald's budget." I laughed.

"Yeah, some of us are, but it looks like you straight," she replied, nodding her head towards the burgundy E Class Mercedes idling at the curb.

What could I say? My nigga was touching real money, but I liked having my own because I was who my son depended on.

Blowing her a kiss, I grabbed my food and headed out the door into the cool summer breeze. It was already 10pm, but it seemed like everybody and they momma was out in the streets.

Before I got to the car, the driver side door opened. Cam stepped out holding a single red rose towards me.

"What's this for?" I asked after a quick taste of his lips.

"Just because its Thursday, baby," he replied, pulling me in for a more passionate kiss, that had everything tingling in my body.

He took the bag from my hand and held the door for me to get in the driver's seat. I loved driving his car because it rode like a cloud, but with the 22 inch rims, TV's and custom paint job, I knew it had set him back a decent six figures. He always insisted it wasn't anything though, so I climbed my happy ass behind the wheel. Once he was riding shotgun, I pulled off and flowed with traffic through the city.

"Are you spending the night with me?" I asked.

"I planned too, but I got a call while I was waiting on you to get off, and I gotta go handle some business."

"Oh," I said, disappointed.

"If you need me though you know the business can wait, baby. Them niggas know who come first in my life, but I can prove it if you still don't believe me."

I smiled and looked over at him, knowing what he was getting at because he'd been making slick comments for months about making an honest woman out of me. I could be honest and admit my love for him, but marriage? Nah, Slim, not right now.

"I know your priorities are straight, babe, when will you be back?" I asked.

"Sometime this weekend," he answered.

"Can you bring one of your level headed homies with you?" I asked.

This caused him to laugh and damn near choke on his sandwich, because he was forever telling me that his homies were nuts. "Tell me why before I agree to anything," he replied.

"I wanna set up a double date for us and Anisha."

"Okay, that's cool, I know just who to bring," he said.

"Baby…"

"Trust me!" he said, laughing at the skeptics on my face.

I had no choice except to honor that request, but he knew I'd show my ass if things weren't straight. I knew my little man was at home fast asleep, so we just cruised around the city talking about everything and nothing. Conversation with Cam was never forced and that only happened when you had two people comfortable in their own skin.

By midnight we'd made our way to the alley behind my aunt's house on Georgia Ave., listening to Jagged Edge and smoking a blunt.

"I've got a surprise for you," he said around a mouth full of smoke.

"Oh yeah, what's that?"

"You'll have to wait until I get back," he replied, sneakily.

The look I leveled at him was meant to make him talk, but instead he laughed and passed me the blunt. I hit it twice and put it in the ashtray, figuring a different strategy might be in order. I unbuttoned the top three buttons on my work shirt, just enough for him to see my big titties trying to leap out of my Victoria Secrets bra. I could see the interest in his green eyes, but I wanted more so I unbuttoned the shirt all the way, and accidentally hit the clasp in the front that held my bra together.

As my titties bounced free, I could hear the sharp intake of his breath, and feel him already touching me even though his hands hadn't moved. Unbuttoning my slacks, I wiggled them down over my hips and slid them completely off, leaving me with just my white lace panties on.

"What's my surprise?" I asked innocently.

"Huh?"

The look in his eyes wasn't just interest anymore, it was fascination. Having LJ hadn't hurt my body in the slightest; it just gave me a reason to step my game up. Between crunches and Kegels, a bitch was tight all the way around. Pulling my panties to the side I stuck my middle finger deep inside my hot, wet pussy and pulled it back out, making sure you could see my juices glistening in the moonlight, before I stuck my finger in my mouth and sucked them off. I heard the involuntary whimper deep in his throat, and I knew I almost had him. I stuck my finger back inside me, and moved it around for good measure before pulling it out and sticking it in his face.

"Want some?" I taunted.

The speed with which my finger disappeared in his mouth made me gasp, but the way he drank my juices made me wetter still. Before I could stop him, it was his fingers inside of me, and they were hitting every spot he knew I liked. I stuck my hands in his shorts, grabbing his throbbing dick, and freeing it as I climbed into his seat where I could imprison it again.

"Baby wait," he said, using his other hand to fumble for a condom because we both agreed on smart sex.

"You better hurry," I whispered stroking his dick and rubbing it back and forth across my pussy lips.

"Oh, God," he panted, finally getting the gold wrapper off.

He pushed the condom over the head of his dick and I rode that mufucka the rest of the way down. When we kissed I could taste myself on his tongue and that turned me on to the point that I bit his tongue a little.

The whimper in his throat was now a full-fledged growl as his hands gripped my firm ass cheeks, and pulled me down while he pushed up inside of me. Faster I rode him, loving the way we fit together, and the scent of our sex in the air. I could feel his nails digging into my ass which meant he was about to cum, so I slowed it down a little and swirled my hips.

The feeling of him bouncing off every wall inside me made me cum in a great wave, but still I wanted more. Grabbing my titties, I shoved them in his face, loving how he alternated between licking my nipples and biting them, but never missing a stroke of putting that good dick to me. I felt my climax building again so I rode him harder, rising higher, and falling faster until all you heard was my pussy talking that talk.

"Baby not yet," he pleaded.

"Tell me-what I-wanna know," I replied licking his ear lobe, as I felt the familiar shaking begin in my body.

"Car!" he yelled, holding onto my ass while I pushed us both into an atmosphere of orgasmic heaven. God it was intense when we came together, but what I loved most was that his dick didn't just go limp like most niggas. He was still good for another round.

"Wanna take this to the backseat?" I asked, kissing him on his neck.

"Definitely."

Reluctantly, I rose all the way off his dick just as someone tapped lightly on the rear window. Cam slung me into the driver's seat and his all black 9mm Rugar appeared out of nowhere. You couldn't see through the tint in his car, but I could just barely make out a little figure standing by the bumper on the driver's side.

"Hold on babe," I said, grabbing my pants and wiggling into them, while trying to button my shirt. "Put that away," I said.

"Nah, Slim, who is that?"

"It looks like my Aunt Florine, and I was talking about your dick not the gun."

"Oh," he said adjusting himself.

I rolled the window down a little and she stepped forward out of the shadows.

"I wanted to talk to you before I went to bed, but I didn't know how long you'd be out here," she said, adjusting her position so she'd be downwind of the pussy and weed aroma escaping the car.

"I'm coming in now, auntie," I said smiling sheepishly.

Without another word she turned and headed back towards the house.

"Wow, did we really just get caught?" Cam asked, laughing.

I had to laugh with him even though I was embarrassed.

"It's cool, she knows I'm grown," I said, making light of the situation.

"If you say so. So, I'll see you when I get back?" he asked.

"You better nigga! And thanks in advance for the car," I said, kissing him softly.

"Can't believe I told you that."

I laughed at him, grabbed the McDonald's bag and stepped from the car.

"Call me tomorrow so I know you made it to Baltimore safely," I called back.

"I gotchu, Slim. Tell LJ I said what's up."

"I will, nite boo," I said.

"Nite, babe," he said back.

I hurried across the backyard and into the house where I found my Auntie sitting at the kitchen table. After putting LJ's food in the refrigerator, I sat down across from her, noticing the worry lines furrowing her brow.

"What's wrong Auntie?" I asked.

"You got a message today," she answered lowly.

"From who? And where is it?" I asked again.

"It's from Zo, and it came in the form of two gentlemen sitting on my front porch when I got home."

My heart hit my toes at this revelation. I hadn't exactly hidden from Zo, but I hadn't given him my direct location either. Him finding me was unsettling, especially because I was just starting to believe in happiness again.

"What did they say?" I wanted to know.

"That Zo will be in court tomorrow and he wants you there," she replied.

"I'm spending the day with LJ tomorrow so..."

"Baby, this wasn't a request," she informed me.

Part of me already knew that because he wouldn't have sent his homies for any other reason. He wanted me to see that when he wanted something he still got it, by any means.

CHAPTER TWELVE
All Surprises Ain't Good

Normally I would've crawled into bed with LJ and snuggled up, allowing his little kid smell to put me to sleep, but I knew sleep wasn't coming no time soon tonight. On some real shit, Cam had that dope dick that could have a bitch's eyes instantly heavy after climax, but not even my session with him was the cure to my insomnia.

I lay awake until the sun rise and then took a blistering shower with hopes of clearing my head. But, even now, as I sat in the parking lot of the D.C federal court building my thoughts were still scrambled.

What was so important that this nigga wanted to see me now? I thought. For two whole years he hadn't requested or demanded my presence, yet it was obviously important if he tracked me down. He hadn't flexed his muscle for no reason. I wondered how different he would look now. It was guaranteed I was different than he remembered, starting with the fact that micro braids had replaced my once golden locks. Shaving my head had felt like shedding my skin, and that's what I'd been striving for in order to start over. I also did it because I knew how much he loved my hair. It didn't matter how I looked or how he looked, I was just here to find out what the fuck he wanted and then I was gone.

"Well, bitch, you can't do it sittin' in the car," I said to myself, finally screwing up the courage to face my past life.

I stepped out of my car and smoothed out the wrinkles in my black thigh length dress, praying I didn't stumble in my high heeled open toed sandals. It was only 8am, but the entire courthouse was swarming with people and activity.

After making it thru the metal detectors I just stood there, feeling like a passenger at Grand Central Station, while everything moved with purpose around me. I had no idea where I was going, and I was about to ask the desk clerk sitting to my right when I felt someone grab my arm.

"It's been a long time, Mac," C-Will said, steering me down a long hallway that had a lot of doors with the words *Attorney Visit* written on them. I didn't speak, nor did I struggle, but if this nigga acted a fool he best be prepared for me to do the same.

"Relax, Slim, we all came through the metal detectors," he said snickering. At that comment I did jerk my arm away from him, which made him laugh harder.

"Second door on the right from here," he said, sitting on one of the wooden benches that were spaced a dozen feet apart along the marbled hallway.

I followed his directions until I came to the door, and after a deep breath, I twisted the knob and walked in. The room was no more than eight by ten feet, with a metal table in between client and attorney. But with Zo in it, it felt like a shoe box.

Evidence of his dedication to his workout regimen was in the veins that stood out all over his arms and hands, and he was definitely bigger than I remembered. Our eyes met and he gave me that lazy grin, which made my heart stop, and my throat close a little. And though I'd die a horrible death I admitted it, it made my pussy tingle a little too.

"Let me talk to her real quick," he said to his lawyer, but never took his eyes off me.

It wasn't until then that I even noticed the petite red head sitting across from him, but once I got a look at her face I couldn't help feeling she looked vaguely familiar.

"Court will begin shortly," she said, leaving us alone in the room.

"You can come closer, Mac, I'm handcuffed see?" he said teasingly, lifting his bonded wrists.

I sat in the still warm chair the lawyer had vacated and stare at the man who was the cause of my greatest joy and my greatest pain.

"How you been, Mac?"

"My name is Makayla."

This time he chuckled, but lifted his hands in surrender, sensing my impatience.

"How you been, Makayla?"

"Just fine, Lorenzo. Happy actually, and you?"

"Content for the most part, but happiness seems to be only a breath away. You look good, Slim."

"Did you summon me down here to tell me things I know, or was there something of importance to discuss?"

I saw the flash in his eyes instantly, and I knew that would've probably been the moment when he slapped me or even worse.

"How's my son?" he asked.

"My son is fine, healthy and happy," I answered in one, short response.

"I wanna meet him," he said.

I had some slick shit on the tip of my tongue to say, but being a good mother meant I made the best decisions for my child. LJ deserved to know his father, even if I thought he wasn't shit.

"That can be arranged," I agreed earnestly.

"When?" he asked.

"Don't push me Zo," I said, eying him with intensity.

"I haven't pushed you, not for two years. And you know I could've," he replied seriously.

There was no need to acknowledge the truth in what he said, so I chose to refocus on the issue.

"What did you summon me for, Lorenzo?"

"Well first off to apologize," he stated.

"What?" I couldn't believe my ears.

"You heard me, although by the expression on your face I can tell it's the last thing you expected."

Truthfully, I'd expected to go bobsledding through hell first, but I was glad to have a front row seat to this shit!

"Apologize? For?" I asked.

"Makayla, I loved you, hell I still do love you, but I treated you all wrong when I got out. I was so caught up on getting back what I lost, I actually lost the best thing I ever had. I know that now, just like I know this apology can't make up for all I put you through. I am sorry though. I need to apologize for you getting arrested over my dope. And I need to apologize for Teshia because that shit was foul on both our parts. We never discussed it, but I'ma tell you that it was a one-time thing, and it only happened because she was fucked up about KP. Does that make it right? Hell nah, but that's what it was. What I'm apologizing for is that you're out there raising my junior on your own, and I should be helping you," he said.

"Our son is good, Zo."

"Not with you working at no fucking McDonalds, he ain't."

That comment made me wonder just how much this nigga knew about me because he had a lot of particulars for someone locked up.

"He has everything he needs, Lorenzo, and he's a happy child," I added for clarity.

"No doubt, but he's my first born and that means he deserves nothin' but the finest of everything."

"Why the sudden concern now, Zo?" I asked, getting more frustrated by the minute.

"I've always been concerned, but for a while I thought you were the one who told the cops where I was, and I had to figure out how to deal with that."

"I'd never..." I started but stopped.

122

"Save your breath, I talked to Mr. Goldstein so I know you had just got out. That's his daughter representing me now."

"She looks like him," I said recalling his facial features.

"Right. Anyway, I tried to give you space and time to get your legs back under you, but you still haven't. Time's up," he said in a demeaning tone.

"What's that mean?" I asked unsure of his logic.

"It means you're gonna accept my help, period."

"And if I don't?" I asked just to be defiant.

His response was to smile at me, but it was a smile void of all warmth, and it sent a shiver down my spine.

"Next question, Slim," he replied.

"Why won't you believe we're straight? I'd ask you for help if I needed it," I said honestly.

"Really? Like you ask your boyfriend, huh? Why you so surprised, Slim, you thought I didn't know you was sleeping with the enemy? Or are you surprised I know you well enough to know you won't ask no nigga for help?" he said arrogantly.

He was actually right on both accounts, but what really had me fucked up was he hadn't tried to hurt me in any way, for fucking with a blood.

Listen Mac, you're a grown woman so who you fuck ain't my concern, but LJ is my concern. Now I know you ain't been checkin' it, but there's plenty money in the P.O. Box. I actually had to get a few more at the same locale, and C-Will will give you the keys before you leave today. I want you to clear them out, and I want you out of your aunt's by Monday," he more or less ordered of me.

"But..."

"Zo, you're up next," the lawyer said, sticking her head in the doorway.

123

He stood up and moved around the table until he was towering over me. "I promised to take care of you and that's what I'ma do, so save your arguments," he said.

"I will if you answer one question," I replied.

"What?"

"Since you know it wasn't me who told on you, what did you do to the one responsible?" I asked in fear of his answer.

Throughout the whole time we'd been talking I saw some semblance of the love he used to have for me swimming in his eyes, but the look he turned on me now was utterly cold.

"Go see Success if you really wanna know what happens to disloyal, talkative bitches," he whispered in my ear.

I didn't know what to say to that, or if I wanted the answer bad enough to go find out. I stood up to put some distance between us, and opened the door to make exiting easier on his cuffed wrists.

He walked out and made a right towards his lawyer who was standing at the end of the hallway. I made a move to go left, but C-Will stopped me first by handing me a key ring with three keys on it, and then nodding for me to follow Zo.

"Zo?" I called out so he could get his goon.

"Oh, that conversation we had wasn't why I wanted you down here," he said smiling. "Come on, it's almost over."

"I didn't know what he needed or expected me to do in a courtroom, but I followed his lead and sat in the back while he went to the defendants table.

"Good of you to join us, Mr. Thompson."

"My apologizes your honor," he replied.

"Council proceed."

"Your honor in the case of the District of Columbia VS Lorenzo Thompson the prosecution has reluctantly agreed to nonprocess the case due to lack of sufficient evidence. However, should the evidence arise we will be prosecuting Mr. Thompson

124

to the fullest extent of the law there were several people in the gallery who were surprised and downright outraged at what they'd just heard. All I could think was, of course he'd beat a murder charge!

"And what about the parole violation he incurred for leaving the jurisdiction without permission?" the judge asked.

"We've agreed to time served on that offense your honor," the prosecutor replied dejectedly.

"Well then, from the looks of things, Mr. Thompson, you're a free man. But when I see you again, and I'm almost certain that I will, I'm gonna give you every single day I'm allowed to. Do you understand?" the judge asked.

"Perfectly," Zo replied, and even though I couldn't see his face I knew he was smiling that shit-eatin' grin of his.

"Case dismissed!" the judge said banging his gavel.

And just like that, Lorenzo Thompson was free. They took the cuffs off of him and he strolled down the aisle to where I was seated, ignoring the dirty looks coming from Louie's friends and family.

"That's what was so important my sweet Makayla, and I wanted you to be here to share this moment with me," he said smugly.

"Co-Congratulations," I managed to say around the lump in my throat.

"Thank you. What day is good for you this weekend for me to see my son?" he asked, still smiling.

"I don't –I don't know. I, um, work on Sunday so..."

"No you don't, you don't work at McDonald's anymore. You can go to school fulltime if you'd like?" he offered.

"I, um, just give me a minute to think OK," I said, getting frustrated again.

"Take your time. I'll call and leave my new number at your Aunt's house. You got 24 hours to use it, or I'll be the one on your Aunt's porch, understand?" he said, the smile now gone.

I didn't trust my voice and so I just shook my head.

"Oh, and don't forget to pick up that money because I meant everything I said to you, Slim."

And with that he sauntered out of the court room, leaving me speechless and utterly confused. It was easy to avoid a man, if not forget him, when he was locked up, but how did you do that when he was free to roam? And why did part of me want to jump into his arms as much as run away from him?

CHAPTER THIRTEEN
If It Isn't Love

Past Future:

The saying is that the past has no future, so I guess that means we're expected to get used to the idea of loving and losing.

The part that confuses me lies in the possibility that a chapter's ending doesn't mean the book is finished.

So what if no looking back diminished your chances at a happily ever and you're forever haunted by what comes after this?

Should we really miss opportunity calling because its knocks went unanswered? At the same time it's hard to find your way in life if your vision is full of your rearview.

The need and unexplored, can go unnoticed if your focus remains on what could've been, the doors that should've been opened, but I find that looking backwards can clear the way forward in matter of the heart.

To start anew with love you must first understand you, and what love means so you aren't confused, and needlessly needing an illusion that collapses at a feather's weight.

The fate of the unknown is mankind's greatest fear, which makes waiting on the future, or the past, to reveal itself maddening.

It's infinitely worse when you add in this thing called love, making me despise even the taste of it on my tongue. I whisper prayers in hopes that I'm not undone by loving what I can't have.

I thought I had it once, but it seemed to crumble beneath my embrace, unable to last in the time capsule. But did time elapse too soon and should space be made for him to reclaim his place?

True love has no expiration date, so now I must ask if the future is made for my past...or is it the future alone I face?

"Mommyyyy!"

"What is it LJ?"

"Cammmm!"

I hadn't been expecting him so soon, but when I said I needed him he always dropped everything to get to me. Rolling off my bed, I tossed my diary and all its uncertainty into the drawer of my nightstand, and made my way from my bedroom through the laundry upstairs to the kitchen.

My living situation may not have been ideal, space wise, but it was free and it was with family which was why I was reluctant to take Zo's offer, or his demands. Right now I had to figure out how to explain everything to Cameron because he'd never asked about my baby daddy after I explained he wasn't and wouldn't be in the picture. Man was I wrong!

The stairs from the basement led straight into the kitchen where I found LJ sitting in Cam's lap, playing with his huge Jesus piece. Cam wasn't a flashy nigga, but he made both his religious beliefs and his money techniques known with the 30-inch diamond encrusted chain and piece. He even had rubies in the crown of thorns to symbolize blood, and yet he let LJ play with it as if it had come from dollar general instead of Jacobs.

"I'ma take LJ to the store and get him some ice cream," my aunt announced, giving me a knowing look.

We didn't keep any secrets from one another, so I'd already filled her in about my unexpected morning, along with the events that had taken place. I felt so drained after our conversation that I just curled up with my diary and waited for the flood gates to open on my emotional turmoil. Now I had to find the words to explain the shit to Cam.

"Thanks Auntie," I said with a forced smile.

"Here Cam," LJ said, trying to hand him his chain back, but Cam put it back around his neck and told him to wear it.

"Um, I don't think we should walk down the street with that on him," my aunt cautioned.

128

"Nah, y'all a'ight. My peoples out there," he said nonchalantly.

"Your people?" I asked.

"Yeah, when you said you needed me I came prepared for whatever. I told you I gotchu," he said assuringly.

I smiled and my heart beat faster just staring at this good man I had in front of me. A good man was so hard to find, and even with him being down with shit as far as his lifestyle goes, he was still a helluva nigga.

"Y'all good, auntie," I told her.

"Okay, we'll be back in a few minutes," she replied.

As soon as the back door closed, Cam looked towards me expectantly, but I wasn't in the mood to talk.

"Come here real quick," I said, pulling him by his hand so he'd follow me down the stairs.

I led him inside my bedroom and closed the door, knowing we only had about five minutes, if that.

"What's good, baby? What was so important?" he asked.

My response was to pull the black dress I was wearing over my head, revealing my naked body, except for the thigh high heeled sandals I still had on.

"Baby..." he tried to say.

"Shhh, we'll talk in a minute. Right now I need this," I said, quickly unzipping his jeans and pulling his dick out.

Once he saw I couldn't be denied he was down for the cause, hoisting me up against the door, pushing his way inside me. For a brief second I considered pausing for him to put a condom on, but the feeling of his hard, thick, throbbing dick all up in my guts made that thought vanish.

"Bed!" I ordered, putting my legs on his shoulders as soon as my back hit the comforter.

"Now fuck me," I demanded breathlessly, loving the feeling of his weight on me, and the force he was using to pound me.

I didn't wanna make love, I wanted this nigga to tattoo his name on this moose cat. His green eyes blazed down at me with pure hunger, and when he swiveled his hips to get deeper I came hard enough to bring tears to my eyes.

"Harder," I begged, wanting him to make me forget Zo ever existed. Before I realized what was happening he'd flipped me over, grabbed a handful of my braids, and was back laying that pipe before I could catch my breath.

"Oh-oh baby..." I moaned out in pure ecstasy.

"Is this what you want?" he asked, fucking me so hard my titties were upper cutting me in the face.

I wanted to talk shit, but when I opened my mouth he stuck his finger in my ass and I came, squirting this time. Before I could regroup, I felt the heat of his cum explode all through me and I came again. I wanted to keep going until he had nothing left to give, but I heard the door close overhead signaling the return trip from the store.

Shakily, I moved away from him until his dick was out of me, and then I collapsed on the bed to suck in some much needed oxygen.

"You-you wanna-tell me-what-that-was-about?" he asked, gasping for air and laying down beside me.

Where did I begin? The beginning seemed so long ago, and the more I thought about it, the more complicated it seemed. I started talking, slowly at first, but still only cornering the highlights that brought us to the here and now. Cam listened patiently and quietly, not needing to interrupt me once, because he was giving me his full attention.

Once I'd said all I knew to say, I climbed off the bed and put my dress back on, giving him time to process his thoughts.

"So how do you feel about what he said to you today?" he asked, zipping his pants and motioning me to sit on his lap.

"I mean, I understand he wants the best for his son, but he should trust me to take care of him. I've only been doing it since day fuckin' one," I said annoyed at the thought.

"Okay, and you should know being with me means you ain't never gotta want for shit sweetheart," he added as if I didn't know.

"I do know that, babe," I said, kissing his soft lips and wiping the sweat from his forehead.

"So how 'bout this, the nigga wants you to move and so do I, so let's move in together," he suggested, taking me by total surprise.

"For real?" I asked, looking skeptical at his suggestion.

"Listen babe, you know I rock with you and the young one tough, and I want you in my life forever. I know you ain't ready to jump no brooms, but we can still play house," he said, kissing my neck.

"Don't start what you can't finish," I replied, grinding on him a little.

"Then we both better stop. On the real though, you know I got a spot in Baltimore where we can kick back safely. You don't need the nigga money so you can stack that away for Lil' man's education, and gettin' back and forth to meet up with dude for visits will never be an issue," he said seriously.

"Speaking of which, where's my car nigga?" I questioned, rolling my neck and everything.

"Come on," he replied laughing, and swatting me on my ass.

We made our way back upstairs where we found LJ face deep in a pint of mint chocolate chip ice cream.

"That's a nice car you got outside," my aunt said to Cam.

As soon as she said that I couldn't stop grinning because I knew whatever it was my baby had got it for me.

"Mommy car!" LJ yelled momentarily distracted from his ice cream.

"Finish eating, buddy, you can see it later," Cam told him, opening the back door for me to walk through.

What I saw took my breath away. Sitting right behind his burgundy Benz was a matching burgundy, four-door, 2000 Chrysler 300, sitting on chrome deep dish 22 inch rims, and lowered to maybe 2 inches from the ground.

"For real, babe?" I asked, running as quickly as my foot wear allowed to get a better look.

"Of course, and it's loaded," he informed.

When I opened the driver side door I immediately noticed my name stitched into the head rest in black lettering, which was flyy as shit. All the rest of the interior was done in the same burgundy as the car, but it looked two toned. No expense was spared from the CD player, two the TVs in the headrests, to the four six by nine speakers in every door panel, plus the two 15s in the trunk.

"Damn baby, I'ma fuck around and break my windows," I said half joking.

"Nah, Slim, I had special glass put in before they did the tint. You straight," he said laughing at my excitement.

"What about my Lexus?" I asked.

"Give it to your aunt to drive, or your homegirl from work."

"Yeah, I could give it to Anisha because Aunt Florine don't wanna attract that type of attention."

"Okay, yo Cain," he called, and a tall brown skin brother with a lot of tattoos climbed out of his ride. Cam and I met him at the front of my car. "Cain, this is my lady, Makayla. Baby, this is the homie I brought for Anisha."

"What's up, Slim?" he asked, extending his hand to me.

"You from the city?" I asked

"Born and raised in the farms," he answered.

"Ah, a Barry Farms nigga," I said jokingly. Well, you might be a'ight after all," I replied, laughing and shaking his hand.

His smile was devastating because he had the same diamond encrusted veneers as Success', but his diamonds damn near took up the whole tooth.

"So what's the play?" Cam asked, looking back and forth between the two of us.

"LG, bring momma her car keys!" I yelled towards the house.

"Well the play is I'ma clean out that money green Lexus you see parked up the alley, and then we're going to go deliver it to your blind date. After that I'ma leave you two to get better acquainted, because me, my son, and my man have some moving to do," I said with the biggest grin across my happy face.

"Word?" Cam asked.

"Yes, baby," I assured him kissing him quickly.

"Keys, Mommy!" LJ said, handing them to me, and holding his arms out for Cam to pick him up.

Before I could warn Cam against it because of how messy he was, Cam had scooped him up, and took him to see my new car. I gave Cain the keys so he could pull my old car back towards the house while I ran inside to change.

I threw on my red sweat suit that read *JUICY* across the ass and my patent leather black and red Jordan's. Once I had my braids twisted up in a ponytail, I was back out the door in time to watch Cain fighting with the car seat in my new car.

"Why didn't you help the boy?" I asked Cam, laughing.

"He said he needs to practice for when he has youngins of his own," Cam replied laughing with me.

Once everything I needed was moved I strapped LJ in his seat, and Cain got behind the wheel of the Lexus. Cam stood holding my driver side door open for me.

"I'ma deal with my homies and handle business on this end before we leave tonight, so I'll meet you back here about 11pm?" he asked.

"That sounds good, baby. I'll be ready to go by then," I said.

"Call Lorenzo too and work out visitation," he added.

"I will, and I'll open a bank account while I'm running around."

"Cool. I'ma text you in a little while," he said, kissing me softly.

"Okay baby…hey!" I shouted before he was gone.

"Yeah?" he said, turning around to face me.

"I love you, Cam," I said, meaning it from deep in my soul.

"I love you too, Mac," he replied back.

CHAPTER FOURTEEN
Blind Sided

Our first week of living together was a serious adjustment period for all of us, especially since Cam kept irregular hours. But like the man I knew him to be, he made his schedule fit me and LJ so that my son was given a more stable home environment. It was thoughtful things like that which told me Cam would be a great father one day, but we both agreed that day was some time off.

Right now, he was settling in to this ready-made family, and I was settling in to my position as woman of the house. And what a gorgeous house it was! He told me his realtor was a magician, and I believed him because finding a 4 bedroom, 3 bath, colonial style home with over 5,000 sq. ft. with a 2 car garage and sitting on something like 2 acres in east Baltimore, would damn near require a genie.

When I first saw it I thought the nigga was lying about it being his, until he explained to me he didn't hustle because it was cool, he did it to prosper. That was a logical concept, but after knowing so many niggas who hustled backwards, it was strange to see it applied.

I got used to the idea really quick though, and since a bitch was newly unemployed I got on my Martha Stewart and turned our house into a home. It took me six long weeks to get it done, and another week to convince Cam interior design wasn't my calling. I appreciated him respecting a sister's designs skills, but I wasn't doing his whole crews' houses. It was hard work! But I couldn't complain, because now my hard work was being rewarded with a weekend getaway with just me and my baby.

LJ had spent enough days with his dad to be comfortable with him, and so they would be spending their first weekend together just as soon as I took him for his 18 month check-up. I wouldn't be running late now if I'd had the good sense to move his pediatrician out of D.C when we'd left, but Dr. Voss had been seeing my little man since he was born, and I trusted him.

All I knew is Anisha better be out front with her shit when I got to McDonald's, or her happy ass was left. It turned out her and Cain had hit it off. Shit, they'd actually been inseparable for the last two months, and I was happy for her. She deserved to be loved because she was a great person, and since her ghetto ass had never been to the beach I decided it was cool to invite them to Ocean City with us.

I couldn't understand how this bitch had lived in D.C her whole life and had never been to Ocean City! Granted, it's in Maryland, but still it's a trip that everybody made.

"Mama, music!" LJ yelled excitedly, nodding his head to the Ruff Ryders Anthem. I turned it up knowing he just wanted to bark like DMX, loving how cute that was.

I crossed over off of MLK Blvd. and South Capital St. and hung a right into the McDonald's parking lot, slightly annoyed Anisha wasn't outside. I was just getting ready to blow the horn, when I saw the door to her Lexus open, and her flagging me down.

"What up, heifer?" I yelled through my open window, noticing immediately she looked a hot mess.

"Hey." She responded dryly.

"Damn, what's wrong?" I asked.

"I don't know, girl, I woke up this morning and puked like I'd been out all night drinkin'," she replied.

"Well, were you out drinkin'?" I asked.

"All I been drinking is cum, and it's so good for a bitch's skin!" she said laughing.

"Nasty winch, that's why you can't hit my Blunts now," I replied, laughing too.

"Like you won't suck a birthmark off a nigga's johnson, bitch please," she chuckled.

"Touché," I said, still laughing, "put your shit in the car and let's ride, I'ma hella late for LJ's appointment."

I popped the trunk so she could drop her suitcase in, and once she had her car locked up, she hopped in beside me and I pulled off.

"Hey LJ!" she said, blowing him a kiss.

"Auntie!" he screamed at her, showing all his little teeth, with his fresh ass.

He was gonna be a heart-breaker just like his daddy, but luckily for me that was many years away.

"Listen, Anisha, if you ain't feelin' good maybe you shouldn't go. I mean there will be other trips and other weekends," I assured.

"I know, but I'm good, Mac, for real."

"A'ight bitch, don't be callin' my hotel room talkin' 'bout the nigga done put you out, 'cause you got sick on him while ridin' his dick!" We both burst out hysterically.

"What-the-fuck-ever, I got nerves of steel when I'm swingin' on the pole, okay?" Again, we both burst out into a fit of laughter. She interrupted our conversing to turn the music down a little, and then turned to face me.

"I think I know why I'm sick, Mac."

"Okay?" I said, waiting on an explaination.

"I think- I think- I'm- pregnant," she stutter the words out.

"I'm sorry, say whattt?" I asked.

"You heard me," she confirmed.

"So, you been lettin' him smash the cookies with no plastic? Really?" I asked, knowing I'd schooled her better.

"I don't need judgment, Makayla, I need support," she said somberly.

"You're right, and I'm sorry," I replied contritely.

"The dick must be amazin' though!" I said, laughing at the way she blushed, before she started laughing too.

"Girllll, it is ev-er-y-thing, you hear me?" I ain't never called a nigga daddy or cooked for one," she openly admitted.

"Hold up, you cooked?" I asked.

"Waffles, bacon, sausage, eggs, corn beef hash, fried pota- toes, scrapple and even asked the nigga if he wanted me to squeeze him some orange juice!" She was really rolling now.

I laughed 'til tears ran down my face, damn near causing us to wreck, as I flew through a red light.

"Nah, uh, Anisha, you ain't whip all that up," I shouted loudly.

"Shittt, a bitch was butt naked with an apron on ready to give Betty Crocker a run for her money," she said.

"Whew, I can't fuck with you right now, you gonna make me crash," I said, wiping at the tears still leaking from my eyes.

"I'm just being real with you, so yes, he smashed the cookies and the cakes, he was up in those guts R-A-W, you feel me? And now I think I might be callin' him daddy for real."

"How do you feel about that?" I asked seriously, knowing how scared and alone I felt when I found out about LJ.

"I mean, I've always wanted kids, but I'm not even 18 yet. What kind of mother will I be?" she asked, showing the fear that I know lived in every young woman at times like these.

"You'll be a great mother, and do you know why?" I asked.

"Why?"

"Because you already understand what sacrifice is, your mother did the best she could do for you without a man's help, and so you know how to give that same love to your child. I'm not saying Cain won't be there, 'cause I'll kill that nigga myself! I'm sayin' you're strong, intelligent and more than capable to give your son or daughter the world," I reassured her.

"God, I hope it's a boy, a girl would drive me nuts!" she stated.

"Right," I replied laughing.

"Will you be there?" she asked, hopeful.

"Every step of the way," I said, taking her hand in my own.

We rode like that for the rest of the way to the doctor's office, talking about baby showers and late night feedings. I even offered to let her keep LJ for a week just so she could get a feel for it, but she quickly vetoed that idea because she was familiar with his shenanigans. He was definitely coming into his terrible two's early.

"I'ma run to the store real quick," she said once we got to the doctor's.

"Okay, bring some C-A-N-D-Y for him because he acts a fool after his shots," I told her.

For the most part LJ liked his doctor's visit, and as soon as we were through the front door he took off towards the kid's play area in the corner.

Dr. Voss' office wasn't that big, it consisted of a waiting area that seated eight, with wall to wall carpeting to match the chairs. The receptionist sat behind a Plexiglas divider next to the door that led to the doctor's office. It was a small practice that gave you an intimate vibe, which I, as a parent, loved.

"Hey Lola, sorry I'm late," I said to the receptionist.

Lola looked like anybody in D.C's grandma with her shinning white hair, and her twinkling brown eyes tucked into her chubby face. But she wasn't for the shit, and I'd heard her take a few parents outside and give them detailed directions to hell. To know her was to love her though.

"It's okay, child. He's running late himself. How's the little man?" she asked of LJ.

"Bad as hell. I'd say it's hard to believe he's almost two, but it's not. The boy is just so mannish!" I said honestly.

"Aw, he's okay. You better enjoy them at this age because once they get their mid fixed on the Thundercat, he'll never be the same," she laughed.

"Don't remind me!" I replied laughing.

I signed in and sat down with an old Ebony magazine, just as Anisha came through the door toting a big bag from Rite Aid.

"How much candy did you get?" I whispered at her.

"Just enough, but I got a few of these too," she said, opening the bag to reveal three pregnancy tests.

"Why so many?" I asked.

"Just to be sure, and because I'm scared, and want you to take one with me."

My initial reaction was to laugh in her face, but the look she gave said she was serious."

"Sweetheart, that makes absolutely no sense. Cam does have good dick, but that mufucka is protected like Andrew's air force base before he gets up in me," I countered.

"I know you're not pregnant, I just want you to do it for moral support," she replied, giving me her best puppy dog look.

"Oh fine, you big baby, come on," I said, tossing the magazine on the table. "Lola can we use the bathroom real quick?" I called out.

"Sure honey, I'll watch LJ for you," she said, buzzing the door open and letting us back.

We walked past her to the first door to the right, which was the one stall woman's bathroom. "Give me one of them," I told her, feeling more than a little foolish,

"Thanks sis," she said happily.

"Uh-huh." Luckily for her I did have to pee because I wouldn't have waited around to make it rain. I tore the package open and pulled out the pee stick. Lifting my sundress up, I squatted over the toilet, because smart bitches don't sit, and I handled business. I managed to finish just in time for Lola to stick her head in the door and tell me that LJ was in Dr. Voss' office.

"Thank you," I replied, flushing the toilet and rushing to wash my hands.

"Here you go, just let both sit for three minutes and one will be negative or both will. Good luck!" I said to Anisha.

I offered with a swat on the ass, and then I was out the door before LJ had a chance to act a fool. From the bathroom I only had to go three doors down and make a left, but I could hear LJ talking a mile a minute before I turned the knob.

"Sorry I'm late doc," I said to Dr. Voss upon entering.

It's okay, Makayla, I was just matching up with LJ," he replied smiling.

Dr. Irvin Voss was handsome in that distinguished gentlemen kind of way, with his creased slacks and gray button up shirt to match the two patches he had at his temples. He had dark brown eyes and a kind smile, and if my momma wasn't a crack head, I would've loved to introduce them.

"So how has he been?" he asked.

"He's been great, doc, just as bad as he wants to be."

"Well, let's check him out," he replied, laughing and pulling out his stethoscope.

For the next 15 minutes. We went through the routine of questions and answers, observations and recommendations, and finally the shots which made LJ a very unhappy little boy.

Once the deed was done we made our way back to the waiting room where I found Anisha pacing a hole in the carpet.

,"Calm down, you know you might be pregnant." I told her, giving LJ the bag of candy to quiet him.

"It's not that, it's not just me though, it's you too," she said surprisingly.

"Now what now?" I said in shock.

I thought she was joking but her facial expression said otherwise. Her response was to hand me both pregnancy tests that read clear as day, we were both expecting.

"Bitch, did you pee on two sticks?" I asked.

"Really, Makayla? Who does that? When was the last time you had your period?" she asked.

"It was just…oh, God! Ohhh, God!" I shouted out.

The last time I'd had a period was when I lived with my aunt, and that was two months ago! I felt light headed, but still I managed to make it back to Lola's desk.

"Lola, I need the doc to draw blood now," I asked in full panic mode.

"Why baby, what's wrong?"

"I think I'm- I think I'm…oh God!" I couldn't even mouth the words.

CHAPTER FIFTEEN
My Life For His

Despite his candy intake LJ was still worn out enough to fall straight asleep once we'd gotten back in the car, and I was thankful for that. I needed the silence to think and process. I had the radio off, the windows up, and the A/C blowing.

Anisha had been quiet ever since both blood tests had come back positive, obviously stuck in her own world of questions without easy answers. I felt for her because she was younger, and her whole life would now change, beyond the scope of her imagination. But, right now a bitch had issues of her own.

For starters, what type of reckless female has a baby by a Crip and a Blood? Sworn enemies, really? Like my pussy was the Holy Grail that could have these niggas holding hands and singing koom-by-ah! The shit I did went beyond irresponsible, it was downright messy, with the potential for a loss of life.

Zo had been tolerant, if not exactly cool with me doing my own thing, but this was different. This was forever. I didn't know what to do, but I knew I had to be the one to tell him because hearing some shit like this on the streets would definitely have him thirsting for blood. I'd already told him I wanted to holla at him for a second when I dropped LJ off, but I was taking the scenic route to get to Northwest, in hopes that the words I needed would come to me.

"What are we gonna do?" Anisha asked.

"I don't know," I replied, seeking my own answers. For starters, I'ma find some way to explain this shit to Zo."

"Explain it to Zo? Hold up, whose baby is it?" she asked, insulting my character.

"Bitch, please, I ain't that messy! The fact of the matter is, Zo is my first and he's a Crip, and he needs to hear this from me."

"Ah, I gotchu, but when should I tell Cain?" she asked.

"Well, I'm thinking we need to put a hold on this trip and you need to sit down with him A.S.A.P."

"Is that why we're all the way over here in Southeast when it would've been quicker for you to go straight to Zo?" she kept on with the questions. I was irritated enough, and she wasn't helping the cause.

"Don't judge me right now. I just need a moment to think," I answered short.

She was smart enough to hold her tongue, but she couldn't hide her smile. We both knew I could only avoid the truth for so long though. We rode the rest of the way to her car silently, both of us consumed by our own thoughts, and the conversations that would take place in the near future.

I got her to her ride, and we promised to call each other tonight to compare how our baby daddy's took the news.

Before I pulled off, I sent Zo a text that I was coming, and he told me to meet him at his club called *The Play House* up town.

I didn't know when the nigga bought a club, but he better know my son wasn't 'bout to be around the bullshit. I wasn't gonna trip just yet because it was still late afternoon, but that was another conversation we would need to have. I didn't take any detours, and I made it to U ST. in twenty five minutes, pulling in the parking lot next to his smoke gray Phantom.

"Business must be good," I remarked, stepping out of my car.

"I got no complaints. I'm just trying to live. You can come back to the winning team if you want, Slim," he said, getting out of his car, giving me the panty dropping smile of his.

"Nah, I can't," I said.

"Betrayal is a double edged sword in this scenario, sweetheart. So I'll forgive you if you'll forgive me," he said.

"You won't forgive me, Lorenzo."

"And why not?" he asked cocking his head to the side.

"Because I'm pregnant," I blurted out before I lost my nerve.

144

I saw his whole body go stiff, as if a blow had been fired at him unexpectedly. It was hard to look in his eyes, but I felt like I had to, and when I did I was surprised because they were dancing with humor. He brushed imaginary lint from his double breasted black Armani suit, adjusted his black tie against his royal blue silk shirt, and slowly licked his lips before cracking that trademark smile.

"Congratulations Mac, are you having a boy or a girl?" he asked.

"I-I don't know yet, why?" I questioned warily.

"So I know what type of gift to get," he replied chuckling.

"Okay, stop being the weird guy because I know you, and right about now is when I'd be everything but a child of God, followed by a blow of some sort."

"Makayla, you think you know me, but you have no idea who I am anymore," he said these words with a smile, but something flashed in his eyes that weren't friendly. It damn near wasn't human.

"Look, I'll show you I have feelings for that matter," he said, reaching through his driver side window and coming back with a sealed white envelope.

"What's this?" I asked taking it reluctantly.

"Something for you and Killa Cam, but make sure you open it together."

"We don't need your money, Lorenzo," I said, attempting to hand the envelope back.

"Please, you insult me," he said pushing my hand away.

I didn't feel like arguing so I tossed it in my purse on my seat.

"Okay, so why did you have me bring our son to the club?"

"First of all, the club isn't open for another hour, and since I had to come pick up some paperwork from my partner, I figured we'd meet here."

"Uh-huh," was my only reply.

"What?" he asked.

"I don't know. You've still got that weird guy vibe going on," I said, still sensing something was up.

"Life is good, Mac. Can't you just enjoy it? We're finally winning!"

"Are we? Because, once upon a time I thought you and I would own the world together. In that second, I saw a chink in his armor and for just an instant the boy I'd loved more than life was back.

"Me too, sweetheart, me too," he replied, stroking my cheek lightly.

The moment we were sharing was suddenly interrupted by a jet black S600 Benz pulling up, and I took this to be his partner. I could still feel the burn of his fingers as I turned away and went to get LJ loaded up in Zo's car.

I put him in Zo's carseat first so he could go straight back to sleep, and then his weekend bag in the trunk. I was headed to my car with the intentions of leaving, when I heard a voice that made my steps falter.

"Say hoe, park my shit and you bitches get in there and get ready to work. Rent is due before the close of business, or you'll be looking for a new spot to rest your weave."

I looked towards the voice knowing who I'd see, and I wasn't disappointed. I should've known Zo would partner up with a pimp to run a strip club, and when it came to pimping, Success knew his shit.

"It's been awhile, Success," I said, stepping up beside Zo.

"It has, but here I am larger than life and twice as nice," he said, doing a full turn to show off his all white linen suit, with the Gucci loafers to match the Gucci frames on his face. All I could do was shake my head.

"Zo, I'll holla at you in a couple of days, and keep my son away from them nasty bitches," I warned.

"Don't judge them 'til you've seen them," he said, gesturing towards the four women walking towards us.

Any other time he would've been right, but as they got closer I saw that I definitely knew two of them.

"You remember Jessica and Teisha don't you?" Zo asked nonchalantly.

The question was stupid and insensitive, and I wanted to slap him for it, but my anger towards the women paled in comparison to how I felt about him.

"Zo, do you love me?" I asked turning towards him just in time to see something like pain in his eyes? Relax Negro, I'm not gonna ask you for a kidney," I said with the same humor he'd just had minutes prior.

"Yeah, why Mac?" he answered.

"So if I wanted these bitches to eat my pussy right now would you make it happen?" I asked.

"You two hoes come over here and kneel in front of her," he barked at them.

They did as they were told without hesitation, but I could see the loathing within them for the road they'd chose to travel in life.

"Makayla?" Zo asked.

I leaned in between the two so they could hear me clearly.

"You reap what you sow," with that I left them kneeling right there as I got in my car and pulled off.

As a woman I did feel some type of way about the way my ex-friend and ex-lover had chosen to degrade themselves. But, as a woman scorned I knew they weren't worthy of my mercy.

I put D.C in my rearview and began the journey home, playing out every way I could think of to break the news to Cam. I wasn't quite sure what his reaction was gonna be, but I knew he'd be a great dad no matter what. And LJ was gonna make a terrific big brother, whenever I got around to explaining to him why I was getting fat.

I pulled into the driveway just as darkness was settling on our house, and I was relieved to seed Cam's car sitting in the garage.

"Well here goes nothing," I said, grabbing my purse and going inside the house through the kitchen door, off to the garage.

"Babe?" I called out.

"I'm in the living room," he replied.

I found him sprawled out on the couch in his wife beater and some black cargo shorts, watching sport center.

"Hey big head," I greeted him like always.

"Hey yourself, beautiful," he said, sitting up to kiss me and make room for me to sit down.

"So, I heard it's just gonna be us this weekend," he informed me.

"Yeah, did Cain call you?" I asked.

Of course, crying and everything. I ain't ever seen the nigga so happy," he said smiling for his homie.

"Good, because Anisha was worried."

"She shouldn't have been, real nigga's do real things. I'm happy too though 'cause now I don't gotta worry about entertaining no one, and I can focus solely on you," he murmured, kissing my neck seductively.

I could feel my body going to that place it always did when he touched me, but I knew putting off our conversation wasn't the mature thing to do.

"Babe…baby wait we need to talk," I said, stopping him.

"So talk, I'm listening," he replied, pulling the strap down on my dress, and letting his lips dance on my shoulder.

"Cam I'm-I'm…"

"Yes baby?" he said.

"I'm pregnant too."

As soon as the words were out of my mouth, I felt his whole body stiffen as he pulled back to see if I was serious.

"You're what?" he asked to be sure he'd heard me right.

"I'm pregnant," I repeated.

"Not possible," he said.

"Sooo possible, that last day at my Aunt's house, remember?" I asked him.

"Not possible. They told me, oh fuck! Not possible!" he said again.

"They? What they? What are you talking about?" I asked confusingly.

"The doctor's said it couldn't happen. Who's the dad?" he asked, as if his question meant nothing.

"Nigga what?" I asked hotly.

"Num, you wouldn't cheat, shit! It's okay though because you could, but no you wouldn't." Now he wasn't making any sense and I was the one confused.

"Wait, was you about to suggest abortion my nigga?" I asked.

"Nah, nah, nah well, nah!"

"Yo, you really might wanna start saying some shit that makes sense, and it better not begin or end with me killing my child!" I told him, ready to punch him in his damn face.

"A'ight hold up, let me get a drink. I'll bring you one too," he said, dashing off in the direction of the kitchen.

Who would've thought Zo would take the news better than this mufucka! I was beyond pissed, and now I was scared and confused. I really didn't wanna take on two kids by myself before I was 21 years old. I had almost $200,000 in the bank, but it took more than money to raise a child.

I was getting ready to ask what was taking so long until I heard the sound of heaving before vomit hit the toilet water. This nigga is actually getting sick!" I said aloud to myself. That was too much.

I grabbed my purse intending to get my phone and call Anisha, when my hand brushed the envelope Zo had given me. Right about now I was hoping he filled it out with dead presidents, but when I tore it open it contained two pieces of paper and a stack of pictures.

I immediately noticed Zo's bad ass at a young age, and it was some light skinned kid with him. Flipping through the pictures revealed a continuation in theme except the two boys were getting older. By the time I got to the last picture I knew exactly who both men were. One was pointing an AK-47 at the camera with a blue bandana tied around the barrel, while the other pointed a Tech-9 with a red bandana around the grip. When I flipped the picture over, I could hear my heart beating in my ears as I read what was written: *Cousins by blood, never separated by anything.*

If this was true then that meant Cameron and Lorenzo were family, they were cousins. If this was true then both of them had known who I was the whole time, and they'd played me.

"Oh God," I mumbled, feeling like I was gonna faint.

I needed answers, I needed the truth, but this weak mufucka was still in the bathroom throwing up. I turned my attention to the forgotten pieces of paper and opened the one that said read me.

Makayla, how far do you think I'd go for revenge? How long do you think I could wait to see justice served? I told you long ago that loyalty wasn't an option, but you still left me to rot in jail. You left me for dead, now I'm returning the favor.

I didn't understand what I'd done to hurt this man so much, I mean, all I'd done was love him. Had I left him? Yes, but only after he'd cheated with my best friend! Was I not supposed to draw the line somewhere and have some self-respect? I didn't realize I was crying until my tears stained the paper.

I knew there was more because there was another letter to read, but as I opened it and read it, I knew if it was real and true there was no way to prepare myself. There was no consolation. I read it a second time before sitting it on top of the pictures and going into our bedroom.

In the nightstand on Cam's side of the bed was where he kept his favorite pistol, a wood handled chrome .45 with hollow points in it. I grabbed the gun making sure the 16 round mag was full, the safety was off, and there was a bullet in the chamber.

When I got back to the living room he still wasn't there, which gave me time to grab my phone and call Zo.

"Hey Mac, what's up?" he answered cheerfully.

"Is-is it true, Zo? Do you really hate me this much?" I asked, hating the fact that I couldn't stop the tears from rolling down my face.

"I don't hate you, Makayla. I thought I did until today, but I don't."

"So, is it true?" Long seconds of silence passed with no answer, making my heart hurt more with each breath I took.

"Is it?" I asked, almost pleading for an answer. I screamed into the phone near hysteria.

"Yes," he whispered through his own tears.

My son will never forgive you, and before I leave this earth he will know everything you've done," I said.

"Makayla-."

I dropped my phone, picked up the letter and read it for a third time.

"Damn babe, did I react that bad that you had to go and get my gun? I was just shocked because-."

"Because getting me pregnant wasn't part of yours and your cousin's plan? Or, because having a baby with HIV was something you never considered?" I asked. I'd finally reached my boiling point.

"Huh?" he choked out with terror in his eyes.

"There's pictures of you and Zo growing up thick as thieves, and a letter I'm holding from Greater Southeast Hospital that says you've been HIV positive since the mid 90's, tell me it's all a lie, Cam. Please, tell me it's a lie," I begged.

The terror in his eyes was replaced by guilt, sealing his fate as much as it did mine.

"So you fucked me knowing I'd be infected? You came around my kid and pretended to love us knowing you'd sentence me to die! Why Cameron? All I did was love you, so why do that to me and-and my son?" I asked. "Why would you do that me?"

"Baby, I'm sorry, Zo gave me half a million and it was Zo's plan and-."

"Then you can thank him when you see him again," I said firing off shots.

The first two shots took him off his feet and into the wall by the TV, the 3rd shot made him crumble to the floor. I walked over to him and kicked him over on his back so I could look him in his eyes one last time.

Taking aim at his face, I pulled the trigger until all you could hear was metal on metal, and then I threw up all over his remains as reality took a hold of me.

Me and the baby I was carrying were HIV positive, which meant the little life inside me was over before it began. And my life was over too.

Picking up the house phone off the coffee table I called the only person left to call.

"911, what's your emergency?"

"He-he killed me, so I killed him," I said above a whisper.

"Ma'am, are you hurt, do you need an ambulance?" the operator asked.

"It's too late for an ambulance, send a coroner or a priest," I said.

CHAPTER SIXTEEN
Pay It Forward

"Makayla Preston, you have been found guilty, by a jury of your peers for the crime of murder in the second degree. Before I hand down your punishment do you have anything you'd like to say to the courts?" the judge asked.

For a moment, my mind went blank and I saw all the things I was getting ready to miss out on. My life was not my own, it belonged to LJ, and I had failed him miserably.

Ultimately, my actions led to my beautiful baby boy being made a statistic because he didn't have a mama or a daddy. Sure, Zo was present in the court room today, but my Aunt had got him barred from seeing LJ three months before trial.

Between my Aunt Doris, my Aunt Florine, and my Uncle Joe, I knew my little man would come out alright, but it still wasn't the same as having me there. He deserved his mother, and I prayed he wouldn't judge me for loving the wrong type of dude, but that he'd take from my experience and be the man his mama was looking for. I'd given him a good foundation; the rest was left up to the powers to be.

There's not a lot of peace you can make with your life in a three-month window, but I'd started the moment I read Cam's test results. And even though I'd held out a slight hope, I wasn't shocked when I learned me and the baby had the big disease with the little name. So really there was only one thing left to do, and I prayed I wouldn't get nervous since I'd never read one of my poems out loud or from memory.

"Yes, Your Honor. I have something to say," I replied standing up. "I am me now. Some would say I'm the epitome of what not to be and what not to do, but those opinions come from those confused on who 'ME' is.

I completely understand their confusion since the illusion I've painted over my true self for all these years is hard to see through. So who am I?

I might be you if you can identify with my truths. I'm a victim of the crack era, not in terms of using it myself, but in the form of its wealth clouding the sound judgment and leadership of my role models.

I've witnessed its soul snatching abilities dull the light and steal the energy from my own mother, yet I loved her still because to feel anything else was a concept too foreign to comprehend.

I'm a victim of close friends stabbing me in the back in this dog eat dog jungle among us, but sadly I adapted, growing fungus-like, until like day and night, the rules reversed and I became the curse on another man's lips for betrayals felt.

I've dealt with abuse in all forms, and I do mean all forms, until the normal treatment for human beings was so lost on me that I thought I'd lost me.

I had no idea how much the reputation of a cycle would cost me until I dealt abuse out myself, making me no different from the drug or weapon's dealer whose wealth supersedes the health or well-being of others.

I've been a victim of crime if for no other reason than for actually believing in a victimless crime. The list of my offenses committed, and the time I spent behind these fences is significant to the lives I've destroyed, so make no mistake because these words are void of glorification.

The above stated is to show relation, and remove all excuses or justification for change because despite the journey traveled and the roads taken, all that's happened still doesn't encompass me! Who I am now, and who I wish to be, are chapters in my books that are being written because change is a constant action, and new facts are factored in with everyday I'm allowed to grow.

My story is no different than a lot of others, but I'm choosing to unfold it in a light where my kid might not have to travel my roads taken, and the fight for his life can be one that he doesn't have to take in his own hands physically.

Thought is the cause of it all, it's what invented me and you and these like us, who wish to be thought of anonymously. You can exist anonymously, you can remain the old you or the old me, but stagnation leads to only one result, ultimately me?

I feel encouraged in growth, so I'll let you share my testimony, and I'll bleed my truths identity..."

Taking a deep breath, I removed the razor I had taped to my swollen stomach and cut a vertical line up first, my left wrist, and then my right.

The screams from everyone in the courtroom were instantaneous, as my blood showered the wooden table and carpeted floor in front of me. I knew no one would grab me or try to stop me because who really wanted AIDS?

The statement I wanted to make was very simple. I did it my way. Turning around I searched for Zo in the crowd of onlookers and spectators, finding him frozen completely and staring at me in horror. I gave him my best smile, one I knew he remembered from all our years together, and then I spoke my final two words to him.

"You win," I said before putting the razor to my throat and pulling the darkness towards me.

To Be Continued...
Kissed By Death
Coming Soon

<u>Coming Soon from Lock Down Publications/Ca$h Presents</u>

TORN BETWEEN TWO

By **Coffee**

LAST OF A DYING BREED

LAY IT DOWN **III**

By **Jamaica**

GANGSTA SHYT **III**

By **CATO**

BLOOD OF A BOSS **IV**

By **Askari**

BRIDE OF A HUSTLA **II**

By **Destiny Skai**

WHEN A GOOD GIRL GOES BAD **II**

By **Adrienne**

LOVE & CHASIN' PAPER

By **Qay Crockett**

I RIDE FOR MY HITTA **II**

By **Misty Holt**

A SAVAGE LOVE **II**

By **Aryanna**

THE HEART OF A GANGSTA

By **Jerry Jackson**

Available Now

RESTRAING ORDER **I & II**

By **CA$H & Coffee**

LOVE KNOWS NO BOUNDARIES **I II & III**

By **Coffee**

LAY IT DOWN **I & II**

By **Jamaica**

PUSH IT TO THE LIMIT

By **Bre' Hayes**

BLOOD OF A BOSS **I II & III**

By **Askari**

THE STREETS BLEED MURDER **I, II & III**

By **Jerry Jackson**

CUM FOR ME

An **LDP Erotica Collaboration**

BRIDE OF A HUSTLA

By **Destiny Skai**

WHEN A GOOD GIRL GOES BAD

By **Adrienne**

A GANGSTER'S REVENGE **I II III & IV**

By **Aryanna**

WHAT ABOUT US **I & II**

NEVER LOVE AGAIN

THUG ADDICTION

By **Kim Kaye**

THE KING CARTEL **I, II & III**

By **Frank Gresham**

THESE NIGGAS AIN'T LOYAL **I, II & III**

By **Nikki Tee**

GANGSTA SHYT **I &II**

By **CATO**

THE ULTIMATE BETRAYAL

By **Phoenix**

DON'T FU#K WITH MY HEART **I & II**

By **Linnea**

BOSS'N UP **I & II**

By **Royal Nicole**

I LOVE YOU TO DEATH

By Destiny J

I RIDE FOR MY HITTA

By **Misty Holt**

BOOKS BY LDP'S CEO, CA$H

TRUST NO MAN

TRUST NO MAN 2

TRUST NO MAN 3

BONDED BY BLOOD

SHORTY GOT A THUG

A DIRTY SOUTH LOVE

THUGS CRY

THUGS CRY 2

TRUST NO BITCH

TRUST NO BITCH 2

TRUST NO BITCH 3

TIL MY CASKET DROPS

RESTRAINING ORDER

RESTRAINING ORDER 2

Coming Soon

TRUST NO BITCH (KIAM EYEZ' STORY)

THUGS CRY 3

BONDED BY BLOOD 2

IN LOVE WITH HIS GANGSTA

Aryanna

FFB 2 8 2019

CPSIA information can be obtained
at www.ICGtesting.com
Printed in the USA
LVHW052315060219
606704LV00008B/127/P